To Josie —
Enjoy.
Evelyn Cay

MW00955641

Also by Evelyn H Lazare

The Ladies Who Still Don't Lunch

The Ladies Who Don't Lunch

A novel by
Evelyn H. Lazare

For my Daniels, real and imagined

The Ladies Who Don't Lunch

There is nothing glamorous about traveling for work. One airport is as stressful and frantic as another. A meeting room in one city is as depressing as another windowless space hundreds or thousands of miles away. The time tagged on to the business trip as a holiday, with no email access, had been a wonderful de-stressor. Still, after such a long absence, it was good to be home.

Unable to unwind because of jet lag and time zone changes, Lauren could not sleep. She turned on her computer for distraction. When 273 new emails downloaded to her inbox, Lauren groaned. She scrolled through them, deleting many offers of miraculous cures to increase the size of her penis and ignoring stock tips that guaranteed to earn triple-digit returns in the coming week. Each time she saw such bunk, she wondered why scammers even bothered sending it out. Did anyone really fall for this drivel?

Lauren tried to clear as much mail as possible. She flagged the work emails that would need immediate attention on Monday morning. She sent short replies to friends and family when that would suffice, but put off answering personal items that required long responses. She was too tired to go into details about her trip.

She seemed to develop a rhythm to her review of the emails: delete, delete, delete, save; delete, save; delete, delete, save. She continued to scroll down the list, increasing the tempo as she tired of the spam. Just as she was about to delete an email with the subject 'memory lane,' she delayed for a nano-second to check who sent it.

At 23, Lauren had spent 20 years in one sort of educational facility or another, from nursery through graduate work. Finally, she was out of school.

Lauren accepted a job offer from one of North America's most prestigious hospitals, Massachusetts Children's. Life looked good. Being out in the working world on a permanent basis was an interesting change. Having a job in hospital management with a serious paycheck attached was great. And not having to study for exams was even greater. On the other hand, she had to remember that this was not just a summer job and that September was not really the beginning of the year.

Her new address was a one-bedroom rental apartment in the redeveloped warehouses on the Boston waterfront. Lauren commuted the twenty-minute drive across town in her new sports car, a graduation gift from her father. The apartment complex was popular with young singles. There was always a party going on, generally starting at the outdoor swimming pool in the warmer weather or in the games room when the weather cooled. The social life in the complex was an unexpected bonus.

It did not take long before Lauren was part of the friendly scene. She was quick to collect a group of acquaintances, male and female, from the building, the hospital and elsewhere.

At the core of her circle of new friends was a small group of women. Louisa, her next-door neighbor, introduced herself the day Lauren moved in. She saw the movers unloading Lauren's things and strolled over to say hello, proffering a bottle of wine as a one-woman welcoming committee. Louisa's apartment was the mirror image of Lauren's. In fact, they slept head to head on opposite sides of a common wall separating their units. This was somewhat nerve-wracking for Lauren, because Louisa was a gun collector and kept a pistol in her nightstand. Lauren hoped that if her neighbor ever needed to use her weapon, she would not aim towards the headboard.

Louisa introduced Lauren to two distinct communities in Boston – one Irish and the other Philippine. Her mother's family was the former and her father's the latter. Louisa, their only daughter among their five children, was an exotic-looking young woman with an innate old world charm. She was always up for a last minute shared meal or movie. It did not take long for Lauren and Louisa to feel as comfortable in each other's apartment as in her own.

Marjorie also worked at Massachusetts Children's. She was more than twice Lauren's age – older than Lauren's mother. A child psychiatrist, Marjorie treated Lauren as her own daughter, or rather she expected Lauren to behave as the responsible young women her daughters had become. Her three girls were a psychiatrist married to another psychiatrist; a lawyer married to another lawyer; and a librarian married to a teacher. All were over-achievers like their mother, even the rebellious one who married out of her profession. Before the word was popular, Marjorie became a mentor to Lauren.

Lauren met Gwen at the gym in the apartment complex. They soon discovered that Gwen's husband had gone to the same graduate school as Lauren. Chris was a few years older and that much further ahead in his career as a CFO for an office supply chain. Gwen was taking time off from her job as a nurse, after the birth of their first child. She and Lauren reminisced about life as graduate students in Chicago, giving them an instant bond. Lauren became a surrogate aunt to Chris and Gwen's first son, giving her the chance to participate in the baby boy's life and giving the young couple some time for themselves. It was a good arrangement for everyone.

Andrea was the final member of Lauren's inner circle of women friends. They had been dorm mates at Berkeley, then lost touch when they went to different graduate schools. A month or so after moving to Boston, Lauren ran into her old friend at the salon when she was having her hair cut. Andrea was working for a law firm in downtown Boston. She lived in an old brick building near the Commons. They sometimes met for lunch at Faneuil Hall's public market, enjoying the famous deli sandwiches. They ate them standing up and bending from the waist so that the sauce would not drip onto their clothes. And they always smiled broadly when they finished, each checking the other's teeth for offending peppercorns and clinging pieces of parsley, before heading back to their offices for the afternoon.

Lauren introduced all the women to each other at a Sunday brunch on her small patio. The menu was mimosas, frittatas, and a green salad, accompanied by a French stick from the market. It also included the strong coffee that Lauren preferred. She made several pots in her new French press – one of the many new gadgets that crowded her galley kitchen. She enjoyed cooking and all the toys that went along with it. Her favorite culinary tool was a feather whisk. She wasn't sure that she'd ever use it, but she liked the look of it hanging from the gadget rack.

Despite their different ages and stages of life, the women got along very well and began meeting about once a month. Lauren enjoyed their company, individually and as a group. Knowing them gave her a sense of connection and rootedness.

Lauren was born and raised in San Francisco. After her parents divorced, Lauren lived with her mother. Her half-brother, from her mother's first marriage, did not move with them. At 19, he felt he was too old and wanted to be on his own. He left San Francisco for Hawaii and lost touch with the family not long after. Essentially, Lauren was an only child.

At the time her parents ended their marriage, shared custody was not common. Besides, Lauren was a young teen, and it would have been difficult to impose a visitation schedule on her. Still, she did see her father at least twice a week. She was quite independent and visited with him when she found time between her other activities, including school, extra-curricular sports and programs, babysitting and hanging out with her friends.

There weren't many kids at her school who lived with only one parent. She did have one classmate whose father had died, but Lauren was unique among her friends in having divorced parents. Divorce just was not common back then. She never told her father what it was like at home after he left. It didn't occur to her to complain. Besides, she enjoyed visiting her father in his new apartment and did not want to bring negativity into their visits.

Her parents had sold the family home when they split up and Lauren and her mother moved to the neighborhood behind Ghirardelli Square. Living in the small apartment that they shared made Lauren feel more like a roommate than a daughter. Her mother worked as a graphic artist for an advertising agency and left Lauren to her own devices a great deal. She assumed that Lauren could take care of herself and Lauren did not disappoint her. What choice did she have? She learned to cook and to enjoy her own company at meal times.

Apartment living was new to her and Lauren considered it an adventure. It also felt temporary – as if she were acting in a play staged there. Lauren liked the proximity of the flat to the water, even if it made getting to school a real expedition. She took the cable car and then a bus to commute and used the time to daydream about the adventures she would have on the motor scooter she craved. She thought it would be a perfect solution to her transportation problems, but her parents would not discuss it. Even when she was old enough to get her license, Lauren's mother and father were adamantly against her two-wheeled dream.

Lauren was determined to leave San Francisco for university, even if it was only to move across the Bay to attend Berkeley. When she finished high school, Lauren won a scholarship to study mathematics there. Her father was proud of her acceptance, although he was not happy about Lauren leaving San Francisco. Her mother seemed indifferent. Both her parents thought she was too young to go away from home and expected her to come back to San Francisco every weekend. Lauren thought otherwise and limited her visits to school breaks and holidays. To be truthful, although she missed her parents, and especially her father, she felt like a stranger when she returned to their apartments, neither of which felt like home to her.

Many of her former classmates and friends from San Francisco were also at Berkeley. Perhaps because there were so many familiar faces, Lauren found college life like a further four years of high school. When she graduated, she felt she did not know much more than she had when she started. Except for one thing: Lauren knew she could not pursue further studies in mathematics. Her experience tutoring while an undergraduate made her realize that she could not spend her life teaching the subject. It was gratifying when some children she helped finally grasped the concepts and lost their fear of numbers. It was also exceedingly frustrating when other children could not understand, no matter how many different ways Lauren explained the functions and theorems that came so easily to her.

"I could always teach at the university level," she told a classmate over coffee at the student union.

"And face students like that guy who always falls asleep in class? I can just see you bringing in an alarm clock to wake him up."

"I guess not," admitted Lauren. "But I do want to go on in school; I just don't know yet what I want to study."

Her inspiration came from an unlikely source. In her junior year, Lauren dated a medical student. When he took on a clinical rotation at Back Bay Medical Center, Lauren sometimes met him for a late lunch if she did not have to rush back to campus for afternoon classes. One day, they took their cafeteria fare outside and sat on the grass to eat. Her boyfriend took a bite of his sandwich and looked up at the sky. "Doesn't this remind you of the Aegean Sea?"

With his mouth full, his speech wasn't clear. Lauren thought he was asking about the A. G. and C. She knew that hospitals were a breeding ground for acronyms and wracked her brain to decipher this one. Acute Gyne Cancer? No. Admissions, Geriatrics and Chronic Diseases? Unlikely.

Her boyfriend looked at her strangely when she delayed answering. "Well, doesn't this remind you of the Aegean Sea?"

Lauren silently tried a few more possible definitions in her mind before she admitted defeat. "Sorry. I don't know what you're talking about," she finally said.

"Come on, don't you remember your grade school geography? Aegean Sea – Greek Islands, blue skies and beautiful water..." Lauren laughed. She was embarrassed and she never knew how to respond to teasing.

The acronym incident piqued her interest in hospitals. She did not like the sight of blood, so medical school was out of the question. And she did not see herself as a nurse; the old 'handmaiden to the physician' thing was not for her. It occurred to her that the management and business side of these institutions might be appealing and that her maths background would stand her in good stead for accounting, finance and the like. The more she investigated hospital administration, the more attractive it became. Through a friend of her father's, she was able to job shadow the CEO of a major medical center, which convinced her that she'd found her niche. With the CEO's encouragement, she applied to his alma mater, the University of Chicago Graduate School of Business. It was the only business school in the country that included a specialty program in hospital administration. Not surprisingly, it had an excellent reputation.

Both the GSB and the specialty program accepted Lauren, prompting her move to the Midwest. Graduate school was entirely different from university. Perhaps it was that she was so far from home. Perhaps it was that Chicago was such a huge city, compared to San Francisco. Or perhaps she just needed to acclimatize quickly, when she experienced her first true winter. Whatever the cause, Lauren adapted very well, even to the weather. She worked hard, making Dean's List almost every quarter. And she played hard, dating students from almost every one of the professional schools. When she neared graduation, several major hospitals tried to recruit her, but ultimately she chose Massachusetts Children's for her first 'real' job.

She was excited to move to the east coast and felt at home in Boston very quickly. It was closer in size to San Francisco and it projected the same ambiance in many of the ethnic neighborhoods. The reclaimed waterfront warehouses, where she lived, reminded her of similar developments on the Bay.

Lauren met Michael at one of the first parties she attended with Louisa at the apartment complex. Michael reminded her of a marionette. He was tall, gangly, and somehow loose. To Lauren, he looked as if his body would fall apart if he weren't careful. He ambled, rather than walked. And he collapsed into chairs, rather than sitting. But it was his chiseled features and his beautifully expressive hands that she noticed most.

Michael was a resident in orthopedic surgery at Boston City Medical Center. They rarely discussed work, except to chuckle over some of the more humorous aspects of hospital life. (Lauren's boss actually ate his ties. Michael often scrubbed in on surgeries with an anesthetist who listened to stock market reports while he worked.) They shared a quick sense of humor, which was one of the things that bound their relationship.

Michael was a native of Boston. He introduced Lauren to many areas of the city, taking her to his favorite haunts and restaurants and inviting her to out-of-the way galleries, bookstores and bars. Occasionally, Andrea and Ian, another young lawyer, joined them on double dates.

Outside the medical center, Michael's passion was flying. He was a part owner of a small plane and flew short trips as often as possible. When he took Lauren flying, she began to realize how much she loved the skies and how very different it was to view them without hundreds of other passengers sharing the cabin. One of the most memorable flights they took was on a glorious day during an air traffic controllers' strike. They had the skies to themselves for the entire trip. It was breathtaking and peaceful at the same time.

Years later, when Lauren took her first (and only) flying lesson, she recalled that experience. Handling a small plane was a paradox. Lauren felt that she was suspending reality and at the same time, putting her faith in the principles of physics. It was a rush similar to none other, until she hit an air pocket and plummeted ten or so feet, breaking the spell. The end of her relationship with Michael was somewhat similar. It was easy going until they hit an unforeseen rough patch. They were too young and too inexperienced to be able to recognize it as such. They could not work through it.

Lauren talked about the break-up over dinner with her women's group.

"How dare he stop seeing you. What is he thinking?" Louisa, who was hosting the dinner, offered to set him straight.

"Keep your pistol in its holster, Gunslinger. We know the answer to that question," Andrea offered. "He's not thinking. He is a man. And all men are boys. Don't ever forget that."

"Right," said Gwen, "It's rule number one in understanding the sexes. All men are boys."

"How can you say that? What about Chris?"

"Lauren, I love Chris. He is a great husband and when the baby is out of diapers, he will be a fully-participating father. But of course, he is a boy. It's just that he's my boy."

Marjorie stayed silent while the younger women bantered back and forth about dating, break-ups and the density of men. She had been through this before, with her three daughters. And she had been through it herself, when she was the age of the women around the table. Finally, they looked at her.

"What can I say? I have no words of wisdom when it comes to men and romance. What I can tell you is that by dint of his choice of profession, Michael comes complete with a surgeon's ego. He's used to being in charge and people usually ask how high when he orders them to jump." Marjorie had their attention now. "And our friend Lauren probably forgot that rule. My guess is that she knocked the prima donna surgeon down a notch or two, probably without even realizing it. And Michael's way of dealing with that was to back off entirely."

"Yikes! Am I that competitive? Surely not with Michael. I mean, when he became chief resident, I took him out to dinner to celebrate. How does that translate into diminishing his ego?"

"Lauren, relax. I am not criticizing you. All I am suggesting is that when two smart people with two healthy egos get together, there is always competition, no matter how subtle. It's something you'll have to live with always, I'm afraid."

"Right," Louisa jumped in. "I can't see you hiding your light under a bushel. It would take a very strong man not to be intimidated by you. And as we have just said, all men are boys. Which brings us right back to where we started."

"Can I suggest something?" Andrea tapped her spoon against her coffee mug to get the attention of the others. "Why don't I ask Ian to talk to Michael? I mean man to man, you know. They've started playing racquet ball from time to time and it might be a way to find out what really is going on."

Lauren was not sure it was such a great idea, but agreed when the others encouraged her to do so. She thought Ian a little strange but never said anything because she did not want to hurt Andrea's feelings. Ian flashed his money around a lot, as did many young men in those days. But it was his intense sense of privacy that was particularly off-putting. He never answered a question directly or said much of anything at all. He just seemed to observe others. It was as if Ian took notes about Michael and Lauren, to see how relationships worked. He was almost voyeuristic that way.

Ian's efforts did not bring Lauren and Michael back together as a couple. They did remain friends though, even if they no longer dated. Friends with benefits. It would have to do.

Lauren was not surprised that after she moved to Chicago, Michael called to ask whether he could come out for a visit. She was surprised that Ian wanted to come along. The three of them enjoyed a fun-filled reunion, with Ian still quiet and staying somewhat in the background. Chicago offered many attractions and sights to explore and Lauren was in her element playing tour guide. It was good to be back where she had gone to graduate school and she was proud to show off her adopted city.

A second visit followed the first. There was something peculiar about having Michael drop in and out of her life, but they fell into a pattern of skimming the surface of their earlier relationship and enjoying their brief reunions, in and out of bed.

They never tried to resurrect their romance, which seemed to work well for both of them.

Not long after their second visit, Lauren left for an international conference and a visit to WHO headquarters in Switzerland. On her first stop, in London, she became very ill with pneumonia and was admitted to hospital for some time. Lying in a hospital bed in a foreign country was frightening and stressful. Lauren put Michael and Ian out of her mind and focused on regaining her health. After her discharge, she spent several weeks recuperating at the home of relatives who lived in Brighton.

Lauren never travelled to the WHO in Geneva. More than a month passed before she was back in Chicago and another three weeks went by before she could return to work full-time. When she finally did, her boss called her into his office.

"Welcome back, Lauren. I know you are passionate about international patients' rights, but don't you think you took it a bit far this time?" Alan Forester, President of the American Patients' Rights Association, possessed a very dry sense of humor. Lauren never knew how to respond to his comments. "Be that as it may, your experience as a patient in the National Health Service in the U.K. should serve you well in your new post. I have decided to promote you to Vice President of the APRA. Long overdue, actually. Congratulations."

Lauren was delighted with her increased scope of responsibilities. One of the issues she felt very strongly about was the design of inpatient treatment facilities. Briefly, Lauren's theory was that architects designed these buildings for the health care professionals who worked there, with little regard for the patients. To overcome this imbalance, Lauren spent a lot of time working with architectural firms specializing in hospital design. She never tired of telling them that the environments they created could have a positive impact on healthcare outcomes.

Sometimes, the architects and designers who had been patients themselves understood this.

Richard Walker was one of them. He was an architect who sat on an APRA task force charged with developing a patient-centered planning model for community hospitals. Lauren was impressed with his approach to hospital design, discovering much later that his views had first formed when he spent several months in hospital as an adolescent.

After falling during a physical education class, Richard had developed a sore hip. When it did not heal, his parents took him to a specialist who ran innumerable tests before ultimately diagnosing osteomyelitis, an inflammation of the bone that was eating away at the ball and socket joint. There was no known cause and no known cure at that time. The treatment was to immobilize the joint. Richard endured a full body cast, reaching from his shins to his armpits. He was 12 years old, a difficult time to ask a boy to sit still for a few moments, let alone to lie in a hospital bed for weeks on end.

Fortunately for Richard, the condition ultimately responded to treatment and reversed itself. He left hospital with few lingering after-effects. But the memory of the boredom he experienced stayed with Richard. When he became an architect, he was determined to change the experience for other patients. He frequently commented that at the very least, patient rooms should be designed so that the patient could look out the window, rather than onto a blank wall or into the corridor.

Richard argued that interactions with the staff took up perhaps a total of two hours a day, but patients remained in bed for the other 22 hours as well. From that perspective, architects should design patient rooms for patients, rather than for the medical team. Lauren applauded this approach. The medical establishment wasn't always as supportive.

After the community hospital planning task force disbanded, Lauren ran into Richard at an art gallery opening. They were each with a group of friends. After introductions, they went their own ways. A few days later, Richard called to ask Lauren out for a drink. She was a little leery that she might be mixing business with pleasure, but ultimately agreed to meet him at The Palmer House after work.

As she sat across the table from Richard, Lauren tried very hard to steer the conversation away from hospital rooms. It seemed they shared nothing else, which made their time together almost endless. After declining Richard's invitation to turn drinks into dinner, Lauren took a cab back to her flat in Hyde Park. She kicked off her shoes when she returned home and shook her head as she relived the evening in her mind. Conversation with Richard was like pulling teeth. It was a wonder they had ever been able to work together.

It came as a complete surprise when Richard called again. He asked Lauren to join him for a screening at the International Film Festival. It was even more of a surprise when Lauren heard herself agreeing to go. Their second date was almost as awkward as their first. When they were at the movie, Richard pulled the pretend-to-stretch and put-your-arm-around-her routine. Lauren almost laughed aloud. She had not experienced a maneuver like that since high school and wondered whether Richard had been on a date since his late teens. Her curiosity increased as Richard shook her hand at the door when he brought her home after the film.

It was their third date that was the watershed for Lauren. Richard took her out on Lake Michigan on a particularly beautiful day. A skilled sailor, Richard worked the tiller and the sails, doing most of the work single-handedly. He left Lauren to sit back and enjoy the sunshine, the beer, and the extemporaneous architectural commentary that he gave as they tacked back and forth parallel to the shore. Her enjoyment increased even more when Richard pulled off his shirt, exposing a handsome chest that seemed to darken from the sun before her eyes. Lauren, whose skin burned no matter how much sunscreen she wore, was instantly envious.

The day of sailing turned into the longest date of Lauren's life. When he took her home this time, Richard's awkwardness disappeared. He ended up staying the night. And the next. And the next after that. Day after day, he moved in more of his things and took over more of her home and her heart.

The evening of their sailing date, Lauren told Richard that she knew she would marry him. It was a startling admission on her part, since they barely knew each other. Lauren described this revelation as being completely out of her hands. She recognized that she spent more time debating which shoes to wear than whether she should marry this man. And even that did not quite explain it.

Richard certainly had not suggested marriage on their third date. Later, though, he told Lauren that he fell in love with her on the second. She never understood that. That was the foreign movie experience. The evening that ended with a handshake at the door. Who could explain these things?

Lauren tried to think about Richard rationally. She failed. Quite simply, he seemed to have stolen not just her heart, but her brain as well. He had come into her very full life, mindless of her active social life, and hit her with a thunderbolt. Lauren had heard that expression somewhere. It was the best way to describe how completely taken she was with Richard. And why, at the same time, she could not describe why or how it had happened.

Did they have anything in common besides hospital rooms? They shared the fact that they both grew up in San Francisco, although in different neighborhoods. They were familiar with the same landmarks and could identify the sites in each other's stories. They understood how the city worked, as only natives could.

Another similarity was that neither of them went back to San Francisco after graduating from university. Lauren was on a plane the day after commencement at Berkeley. She took a summer position at a hospital in Chicago before beginning her graduate work. Richard left to work for an architectural firm in The Loop. The fascinating architecture in Chicago intrigued them both. It was as if the buildings knew they had to be particularly solid to withstand the wind whipping off Lake Michigan. The beauty of the buildings was somehow more impressive because it did not look fragile or frivolous, as was the case with much of the architecture clinging to the hills in San Francisco.

Their love of old buildings led to their first trip overseas. They flew to Italy, where they spent days on end walking down the little streets in Rome and Florence. Ignoring guidebooks and avoiding crowds, they stumbled upon architectural delights that were hundreds, if not thousands of years old. Perhaps by admiring all these long-standing structures, they were trying to draw strength for the admittedly fragile foundation of their relationship. After all, even the oldest structures were once young.

Richard and Lauren's wedding took place two years to the day after their first date.

Lauren and Richard's decision to marry received mixed reviews from both their families. Lauren had long maintained that she was not interested in marriage. To prove her point, she attended family events with a different man each time. Her more conservative aunts and uncles were relieved that their too-smart-for-her-own-good niece was finally going to settle down. Her more pragmatic relations wondered whether Richard was strong enough to be with her. On his side, the jury was also out. Some of his family considered Lauren an upstart, which always made her laugh, as they were only one generation into their wealth and status.

Lauren well remembered her first meeting with George, Richard's father. George looked her up and down and asked her, point blank, who were the five most important men in her life. Lauren was somewhat taken aback by his question and took a moment or so to think before replying, "My accountant, my lawyer, my broker, my father – and your son." That seemed to appease the older man and George and Lauren went on to have a warm relationship.

Richard's mother, Harriet, was another story. She never tired of comparing Lauren to the wife of Richard's younger brother and she always found Lauren wanting. No matter what Lauren accomplished, it was either not good enough for Harriet's son or was unwelcome for putting her other daughter-in-law in an unkind light. Lauren tried her best to get along with her mother-in-law, but grew tired of her social climbing, name dropping and constant harping. What was even worse was that Richard was also the target of his mother's barbs. Lauren could not understand how the woman could treat her own son the way she did.

Richard's sister-in-law, Barbara, was also a thorn in Lauren's side. Barbara never spoke a good word about Richard, Lauren or, ultimately, their children. She did not hide her disapproval when Richard married Lauren, someone she considered beneath him. The final straw came when Barbara told Richard that he should divorce Lauren and marry a proper wife that she would choose for him. Richard and Lauren had been married for over 10 years at the time. Lauren was barely able to have a polite conversation with her sister-in-law after that. It was not just that her sister-in-law was so sanctimonious. It was also that she was so rude to her own brother. Again, Lauren could not understand how one family member could treat another so unkindly.

Shortly before their wedding, Richard and Lauren bought an old house in Hyde Park, planning to update and upgrade it. Richard could see the final product in his mind's eye and he helped Lauren visualize how it could be transformed. Even before they moved in, they made plans to begin renovating as soon as they held title.

Their first project was the kitchen. Richard, who loved to cook as much as Lauren did, was at his most creative with the design. They hired contractors to completely gut, expand and rebuild the original, finishing the work about a week before their small, at-home wedding. It was to be the first of many rounds of renovations.

Their 1920s house began with two storeys, five bedrooms, and one bathroom. It had both an un-insulated attic and a dirt cellar not quite high enough for Richard to stand in. By the time they were done, their home boasted four storeys, three bedrooms and four bathrooms, including a nanny suite in the finished attic and a playroom in the full height basement.

It seemed to Lauren that every time a major event took place in their lives, they renovated. The first round took place in time for their wedding. Not long after that, they redid the second floor, creating a master suite, complete with en suite bathroom and a walk-in closet. The project also included renovating a nursery and third bedroom. Lauren endured all the work while pregnant with their first child, Emma.

Two years later, when she was once again pregnant, they decided to refurbish all the wood in the house, scraping off years of paint from staircases, fireplace mantles, baseboards and chair rails. The biggest part of the project was restoring the floor-to-ceiling bookcases in the large library at the front of the house and redoing all the wood floors. But the result was worth it, even if Lauren and Richard knew that the trend to painted wood would eventually come back.

One renovation project led to another. With all the money they were pouring into their home, Richard suggested that they make the house more energy-efficient by changing the windows, adding insulation in the walls and roof and replacing the ancient octopus furnace in the cellar with a forced air system. The appeal of air conditioning convinced Lauren, as she could not get used to Chicago's steam bath-like summers. But she was beginning to worry about paying for all the work.

Lauren also wanted to rework the ground floor of the house to create a vestibule as a barrier to the winter. Richard was happy to oblige. Somehow, they even found a master plasterer to redo the cove ceilings in the formal dining room. He was almost as ancient as the house and Lauren worried each time he climbed his wooden step-ladder. But eventually all the work was complete, just in time for the birth of their second child, Jason.

Lauren was working full time as an independent consultant to the APRA by this time, which was why they opened up the attic to provide a room for the live-in nanny who took care of the children during the day. Of course, Lauren's mother-in-law was aghast, commenting archly that her daughter-in-law Barbara did not have childcare help. Of course, Barbara was a stay-at-home mother, not needing to work outside the home... Lauren did not have that option. She and Richard needed the money.

In truth, things began unraveling with Richard shortly after their marriage. 'It's just as easy to marry a rich man as a poor man,' Lauren's mother had told her more times than she cared to remember. Lauren disagreed. She thought it harder to marry a rich man because a rich man always expected the bills to be paid. In Richard's case, he did not seem to realize that he should contribute to paying them. He assumed the money would come from somewhere. And Lauren realized early on that she was to be the source of the funds.

That realization was the beginning of a festering and long-standing resentment on Lauren's part. She took her responsibilities seriously and was hurt and dismayed when Richard did not behave in the same manner. Lauren felt that Richard increasingly shifted the financial burden of raising their children and paying the household bills to her. It is true that she enjoyed her work and could not quite picture herself as a full-time stay-at-home mother, but it's also true that she would have liked the option of spending more time with her children when they were young. Being the major and consistent breadwinner did not give her that opportunity.

Sometimes, when she thought about her predicament, Lauren wondered how so many generations of men had been content – or seemingly so – to be the sole support of their families. Didn't those men long for the chance to let someone else take care of the finances, if only for a short while? A rhetorical question, to be sure, but it was one that tested Lauren's faith in the equality of the sexes and the goal of women's liberation. How free was she, if working in a man's world circumscribed her choices? It reminded her of the saying, 'Be careful what you wish for.'

Being the source of income and parenting two active youngsters was a big undertaking. It's not that Richard did not share in the childrearing or the household chores. In fact, he loved to cook, was quite happy to food shop, and enjoyed spending his time in the kitchen. The problem was that he could not see the larger picture. He ignored the things that needed doing if he did not enjoy doing them.

Lauren's theory was that the expectations of his family were too great for Richard. His father, George, was a self-made man who was quite rough around the edges before his marriage to Harriet and her ongoing tutoring in the social graces. George and his brothers had built a small hardware store into a chain of big box home improvement centers that flourished throughout California and then expanded up the coast and east to the Great Lakes. Anyone interested in do-it-yourself projects shopped at their stores. The family constantly reminded Richard how this empire was built from scratch, relying as much on moxie and bravado as on a keen sense of what the market wanted. George expected his older son to go into the family business, as Richard's brother had, but Richard chose a different path.

Richard's interest in architecture came from his uncle. Lionel, his mother's brother, was developing a growing reputation as a residential architect when he died in a horrid road accident. He left behind not just his wife and young twin daughters, but also a sister - Richard's mother - with a serious case of hero worship. To Lauren's mother-in-law, Lionel was the next Mies van der Rohe, deprived of his international reputation by the recklessness of a drunk driver. Whether or not her estimation was accurate was a moot point; no-one could challenge Harriet when it came to idolizing her older brother. When he died in the car crash,

Harriet turned to Richard to pick up the family mantle of architectural prominence that she believed was their due.

With such conflicting expectations, it was not surprising that Richard was ambivalent about his chosen career. His early goal was to be a pediatrician, in part because of his hospitalization as an adolescent. But his parents held other ideas and plans for him, pushing him away from medicine in the belief that he would be better off forgetting his long period as a patient. When his osteomyelitis had responded to treatment, Richard avoided having his hip joint shaved, which would have left him with one leg shorter than the other and a permanent limp. His parents thought that he should forget that narrow escape from a lifelong handicap. To erase that memory, Harriet and George discouraged Richard from pursuing medicine as a career.

Richard put his dreams of medicine aside and studied architecture. He was a good architect, but he had neither the artistic ability to create outstanding design nor the business aptitude to build a strong practice. It saddened Lauren to see her husband go from one job to another, perpetually seeking positions where he would not feel undervalued, underpaid, or overlooked for promotion. It depressed Lauren even more when the lapses between his employment became longer and more frequent, to the point that Richard ultimately gave up hope and stopped searching for work.

As for Lauren, she did not have the luxury of indulging in self-pity for very long. She was a hard worker and could always be relied on to cope in a crisis. With the outward appearance of a perfect marriage, it was hard for Lauren to turn even to her closest friends to talk about her increasingly dismal married life. Raised to be very independent, Lauren continued to work to support the family, recognizing the conundrum that her trail blazing as a woman in the field of health care management bound her to a situation that gave her anything but independence.

With two young children, Lauren knew that it would be very difficult to manage on her own. When she thought of ending her marriage to Richard, she became even more despondent. How could she cope with the total responsibility for her family, knowing that Richard would continue to be in her life at least until the children were old enough to leave home? Whenever Lauren considered the option of leaving or asking Richard to leave, she held back. Ultimately, she realized that life just got in the way. There were the children to love and support, work deadlines to meet, the bills to pay and so much more that interfered with her ability to think clearly about an alternate plan.

The irony was that one of the reasons that Lauren did not want to marry in the first place was that she feared her marriage would end in divorce. Lauren still remembered the chill that descended on her home when her own parents broke up. Although she definitely did not believe in staying together for the sake of the children, she also worried that Emma and Jason would have a hard time dividing their lives between their parents. She knew that they loved Richard and that he loved them. The thought of shuttling them back and forth between her and Richard was simply not an option.

And so she and Richard stayed together, not fighting and not hating each other. But neither of them derived much happiness from their marriage. Of course, it was not all bad. They still enjoyed some good times, usually when they were entertaining or traveling. Then, they put on the brave faces of a loving couple, not giving any indication of the deeper and deeper emotional and financial chasm between them.

Lauren was on a business trip to San Jose. Originally scheduled for two days, the work was annoyingly slow, with the final resolution nowhere in sight. When the meetings broke up early Friday afternoon, the group decided to take the weekend off and reconvene on Monday morning. The lack of progress frustrated Lauren. She debated going out to the airport to standby for a flight back to Chicago. But even if she was lucky enough to beat the afternoon rush hour and fortunate enough to catch an early evening flight, it would still be after midnight when she arrived at O'Hare. She would then have to leave again on Sunday afternoon, in order to attend the early Monday morning meeting.

Instead of flying back and forth, Lauren decided to remain on the coast and use the weekend for a mini holiday. She took the cowardly way out and let Richard know by email. Then, on a whim, she called an old high school flame who still lived in San Francisco. She and Gary had not spoken in years, but the strength of their friendship from high school and beyond always allowed them to catch up almost without skipping a beat. Lauren explained her predicament and before she could reconsider, she agreed to Gary's suggestion that they meet in Carmel for the weekend. Afraid that she might lose her nerve if she delayed at all, Lauren got into her rental car and headed south. She drove directly to the restaurant they had chosen as a rendezvous point. It was less awkward than meeting at a hotel.

Lauren parked the car and went in to wait for Gary. She found a table that gave her a view of the door and sat down, suddenly aware that she was about to launch herself into a situation from which she knew she would not turn back. Although the opportunity had presented itself to her over the years, Lauren had never considered an affair, even for an instant. Why was this time different? She was well aware that this weekend would likely rekindle the romance that she and Gary had shared for many years, before Lauren left for Chicago. After her move, their friendship subsided into occasional phone calls, always with an undercurrent of longing.

The server approached and startled Lauren by asking for her order. She had been lost in old memories of dating Gary. Richard and the children were miles and miles away and would stay compartmentalized in the Chicago-mother-and-wife part of her brain for the next 48 hours.

Lauren ordered a beer and a salad. She was not very hungry, but knew she would feel less conspicuous eating, than just sitting and just drinking. Her food arrived and Lauren picked at the salad without much enthusiasm. The server asked if everything was ok. After a while, Lauren let him clear her plate. She kept her beer and continued to nurse it for at least another half hour. It was not difficult. She rarely drank the stuff unless she was sailing, and then only because on a rocking boat, it was easier and safer to handle a can than a cocktail glass.

Lauren wanted some air. She finally paid the bill and left to wait for Gary on the outdoor patio. When she pushed open the swinging door separating the restaurant from the lobby, she saw Gary there, about to reach for the door handle on the other side.

She caught sight of him with his arm extended in mid-air. She walked straight into his embrace. The two of them just stood there, hugging and holding each other until other patrons broke the spell.

Wordlessly, Lauren and Gary left the restaurant, holding hands tightly, almost as if they were afraid to let go. It was only when they reached Gary's vehicle that Lauren broke away. She headed to her rental car to follow Gary to the hotel.

Gary had chosen an out-of-the-way country inn for the weekend. Without asking, he signed the register as Mr. and Mrs. and then led Lauren up the stairs and down the corridor to a lovely room overlooking the hotel gardens. The moment Gary closed the door behind Lauren, they again fell into each other's arms and moved without speaking towards the waiting bed.

How many times, as teenagers, did they bemoan the fact that they had nowhere to be alone? Amazingly, this was the first time they had been together when they could be certain that no-one would come barging in on them: not parents, not siblings, not roommates. Although they had not seen each other in over twenty years, there was not a moment's awkwardness at rediscovering each other's mouths and bodies.

Slowly, Gary ran his hands up and down Lauren's back, pulling her closer and closer to him. She buried her face in the crook of his neck, inhaling his scent and feeling so protected in that small space. They undressed each other and made love slowly, then lay side by side, turning to gaze at each other and smile. Neither of them spoke. They reached under the sheets to hold hands again, communicating with the tension in their grip, making words unnecessary.

After a while, Lauren slipped out of bed to shower. She came out of the bathroom wrapped in a terry robe supplied by the inn. Gary lay propped up in bed, watching her. He looked so content. Lauren approached the bed, untying the belt of the robe and letting it slowly slip from her shoulders. They made love again, more passionately this time, before falling asleep in each other's arms.

The next morning, the bed clothes were in complete disarray. Lauren and Gary grinned at the mess they had created during the night. This time, Gary joined her in the shower. It had been a long time since someone washed her back for her.

They were ravenously hungry when they entered the inn's dining room for breakfast. After their meal, the first thing on their agenda was to head out in search of more casual attire for Lauren. She didn't want to wear her business clothes all weekend. Gary kept off the main roads as they spent the day shopping and sightseeing. The weather cooperated, giving them many opportunities to stroll through the small towns they passed. Were they pretending they were a couple like the others they saw that day? Or did they just both lapse into the comfort of each other's presence? Lauren was not sure. All she knew was that she needed to keep touching Gary, holding his hand as if her life depended on it. To let go could destroy the trance.

Their day ended at the dining room of a neighboring inn. Even through dinner, they held hands across the table. Lauren barely ate. Her nourishment came from looking at Gary, knowing it would have to sustain her for a long time. He sensed that something was very wrong in her life, but did not ask what it was. He assumed that Lauren would tell him when she was ready. Or perhaps just being together might be enough. He did not know what to say, really. What was he supposed to think when a former love of his life called, unexpectedly, and all but invited him to spend the weekend with her? A married love of his life, at that?

On their second night together, they barely slept, alternating sex with long talks. Lauren did not explain why she had called. There really was no simple explanation. Instead, their conversation revisited familiar territory. Gary talked about how heartbroken he had been when Lauren left the Bay Area for graduate school. He told her about his failed marriage and his regret that he never had children. They reminisced about high school friends. What they did not want to talk about was if and when they would see each other again.

After breakfast on the second day, they returned to their room to make love once more. If this was the icing on the cake, the flavor was bittersweet chocolate. Lauren sobbed quietly. She hid her red eyes behind sun glasses when they checked out. In the parking lot, she hugged Gary once more then cried again as she drove away, heading back to the business hotel in San Jose where she had checked out on Friday night.

"The thing about affairs is that once you've had one, there is no turning back," Lauren announced to the empty car. "It's just a different type of virginity, and you can't regain this kind, either." Lauren did not feel particularly proud that she had slept with Gary, although she was not certain that a weekend together constituted an affair. More like a tryst, it seemed to her. Whichever, Lauren omitted any mention of Gary when she told Richard and the children about her lovely weekend in Carmel.

But the memory of the two days stayed with her, reinforced when Gary mailed her photos taken at the inn. "Thank heavens he sent them to the office," Lauren muttered to herself as she pushed the envelope to the back of her desk drawer. A week later, he called her at work. When she heard Gary's voice, she was right back in bed with him. That strong reaction made her realize she must end the affair immediately, before it became even more complicated. It was not that she was afraid it would end her marriage; her marriage was already on shaky ground. It was that she was not sure she wanted to end her marriage because of Gary.

Lauren wanted to end her marriage because of herself. Spending the weekend with Gary reminded her how good it was to feel truly alive. For so long, she had not recognized the woman who stared back at her in the mirror – the woman with no self-confidence. Lauren was tired of feeling resentful and depleted. There was no question of if she would leave her marriage. It was only a matter of when.

Years passed before the time seemed right. And when it did, it was unplanned and almost anticlimactic. Emma and Jason were both away at university; they were no longer around to distract their parents from each other. One day, over lunch, Richard and Lauren found themselves talking about their life together. Without acrimony, they agreed that their marriage was over.

At first, Lauren believed that she would be much happier without Richard, especially since she had been so unhappy with him. Her dichotomous thinking led her to conclude that getting rid of what caused the unhappiness would render her happy. Wrong. Lauren was miserable. She cried when she woke up. She cried when she drove her car. She cried when she returned home to an empty house at the end of the day. Lauren wondered how the world kept turning and how anything was accomplished, with so many newly divorced people crying all the time.

Of course, gradually, the tears stopped. One day it just hit her. She had a choice in all this. She could be an unhappy person, feeling awkward and almost guilty when she experienced brief interludes of joy. Or she could be a happy person who felt sad and dismayed from time to time. Lauren chose the latter. This decision was the impetus to do something special to celebrate her new frame of mind. She decided on an extended vacation.

It was her second. Years earlier, she had received a letter in the mail that spurred her to give her life a shake. She had been living in Chicago for a few years at that point, working her way up the corporate ladder at the American Patients' Rights Association. The lawyer's letter that arrived informed her of a small inheritance left to her by a childless great-aunt. It was truly a windfall, as Lauren had no major debts that begged to be paid. In fact, at the time, Lauren had no real obligations, personal or fiscal, to hold her back. No-one depended on her either emotionally or financially.

She had never taken a break before. Her path was straight from high school to university to graduate school and then from one job to another, without any time off in between. Even during her studies, she worked at part-time and summer jobs to help pay her tuition and living expenses. Her time had come. The very next day, Lauren asked for an extended leave of absence from work. Then she booked a trip to Greece, where she toured the islands, experienced nude beaches for the first time, and generally enjoyed the sun and lack of responsibility for three months. Her home base was Mykonos, where she rented a studio apartment in the hills above the harbor. It was blissful. She returned to Chicago, arriving during an early snowstorm, wondering when she would ever have the freedom to take off again. Now, Lauren thought that time had finally come.

The APRA could survive without her for a while. No deadlines loomed. Her children were relatively independent and were doing well. And her finances were sufficiently stable to allow her to indulge herself this way. Sensibility and a lingering sense of responsibility deterred Lauren from heading overseas again. This time, she rented a villa in Puerta Vallarta, Mexico, for what she called her seclusion. It was far enough away from Chicago to be a complete break but close enough should she have to return suddenly.

The aptly named Casa de la Mujere was a multi-level home in the old part of town, about a block away from the famous houses joined by a bridge for Elizabeth Taylor and Richard Burton when they filmed *Night of the Iguana*. Built into the side of a ravine, Lauren's villa overlooked an artists' colony. One side of the house was open to the elements, protected only by wooden shutters. A lower level featured a small plunge pool on a tiled patio. And best of all, the villa came with a cook/maid who knew how to be almost invisible. Maria prepared a light breakfast every day. She squeezed fresh oranges from the farmers' market, first chilling the glass, then the juice.

To Lauren, the cold citrus was ambrosia. And the scent of fresh coffee brewing woke her with an unquenchable thirst. The villa was much too large for her, but she relished her solitude. She spent her days reading and working on needlepoint canvases, sitting by the small pool. She ventured out to investigate every silver shop around, finally choosing several bracelets and earrings to treat herself and Emma and finding a handsome ring for Jason. For dinner, she sampled the many restaurants in the old part of town. And of course, Lauren learned to take advantage of the siesta. Although she rarely napped at home, it seemed so sensible to close her eyes at the heat of the day.

Lauren introduced herself to some of her neighbors, an eclectic group of American expatriates. The longer they lived in the sun, the more eccentric they seemed to become. Eager to find out more about her, they invited Lauren to join them for what they called 'attitude readjustment hour' – just another excuse to drink margaritas. Lauren's contribution was the home-made salsa that she asked Maria to prepare.

Lauren was entirely self-indulgent during her stay in Mexico. She slept late, read voraciously, walked the beach for hours on end and never even turned on her laptop or cell phone. The house had a phone that her children could call in an emergency. Otherwise, she was unplugged and unreachable. Her days developed a rhythm of their own, beginning with the wake-up call of the local roosters, alerting her to the smell of the coffee Maria brewed. After breakfast and a few hours of reading or doing needlework, Lauren prepared a simple lunch and usually dozed in the shade by the plunge pool. When she awoke, mid-afternoon, she headed to the beach for a long walk in the surf.

Lauren was not interested in serious sunbathing. Even on vacation, she was too antsy to sit that still. Besides, she enjoyed her walks and she often explored beaches that were hidden from public view. One day, she climbed a sand dune and paused at the top of the cliff to sit and stare out to sea. The sky was postcard perfect, with cotton batten clouds floating lazily and morphing from one shape to another in the light winds. It was mesmerizing.

The sun shone down on her and she baked in the heat. She was grateful for the sunscreen she had slathered all over. Her big floppy hat shielded her face, but the sleeveless top she wore offered little protection for her shoulders and arms. She did not want to burn again. A sudden shadow provided an instant's reprieve from the heat. Lauren turned around to determine what was blocking the sun. He was backlit; he was gorgeous. His face held just a hint of a smile that told Lauren he had been watching her for a while.

She jumped to her feet to leave. She did not want to risk the hustle of a beach bum looking for an older, solo woman. Her friends had warned Lauren to avoid the young Mexicans on the prowl for women they assumed were wealthy and lonely. It was the reverse cougar situation. But when he saw the look of annoyance on her face, the shadow man spoke. Lauren took a better look at him and realized that he was neither young nor Mexican. His speech confirmed her assessment, "You'd better watch yourself," was his unsolicited advice. "Your back is about to go from rare to rarer." Lauren thought his accent was Australian.

She thanked him for his concern and began to descend the dune when he introduced himself. His name was Peter and he was from New Zealand. "I came down here to check on the work at the water purification plant and I took an extra week before heading home. After all, it's a long way from here to Wellington and who knows when I'll be back."

Lauren thought he had a wonderful voice and an endearing way of speaking. She continued down to the beach, at first replying to Peter's questions over her shoulder. Then she paused for him to catch up. "I'm Lauren," she said, extending her hand to shake his "and I've run away from home in Chicago for a few weeks. I think I may never go back."

Peter smiled. "I can understand. But I do have to leave in a few days and it would be a shame to do so without having dinner with you first."

Lauren laughed. "Well, you certainly are direct."

"Well, if that's a yes, then I said the right thing. And if that's not a yes, I can rephrase it."

"Yes," laughed Lauren. "It's a yes."

They agreed to meet at Café des Artistes that evening. The expatriates had recommended it to her - a strangely named restaurant for Mexico, but one with a reputation for wonderful seafood served in a beautiful outdoor setting nestled into a hill.

That evening, freshly showered and dressed in shantung jeans and a silk top in the same soft teal color, Lauren walked down the hill from her house and along the main thoroughfare to the restaurant. What would she do if Peter did not show up? They had not exchanged phone numbers and there was no way to contact each other. What would she do? She would eat dinner alone. She had done that many times before.

Peter was waiting at the entrance to the restaurant, looking very handsome in his linen slacks and crisp shirt, which he wore with the sleeves rolled up. He told Lauren how lovely she looked and gave her a quick kiss on the cheek, before taking her by the hand to follow the hostess to their table. Their reservation was in a little alcove at the very top of the garden. They sat side by side, their backs to the hill behind them and shrubbery on both sides affording privacy from the other diners. Their vantage point let them look down on the other tables. "It makes me feel very regal sitting up here," Peter said with a grin. "I feel that I should be waving to my subjects to acknowledge their loyalty."

There were a few moments of awkward silence, when neither of them knew how to continue the conversation. The waiter brought the wine list and handed it to Peter. While he scanned it, Lauren watched him out of the corner of her eye. It occurred to her that, apart from her weekend with Gary, this was her first time alone with a man since before her marriage to Richard. It was both frightening and exciting and Lauren was determined to enjoy every moment.

"Mexico is not known for its wine selections," Peter commented, putting the menu down. "And somehow I'd feel better supporting the local economy. When in Rome and all that. Even when in Mexico."

Lauren did not know whether he was teasing. "I'm fine with either" seemed like a safe response.

Peter laughed. "And here I thought all American women were radical feminists who would never tolerate a man ordering for them. What a relief."

Lauren still did not know whether he was serious. "Well, I'm happy to see that you're as befuddled by my behavior as I am about yours. So if you are serious about ordering for me, I'm fine. As long as you order a mango margarita for me and another one for yourself."

The waiter, who had been hovering while he waited for their order, jotted something on his pad and disappeared before Peter could speak. He returned in a few moments with a frosty pitcher of margaritas and a plate of olives for them to nibble on. Lauren warned herself to pace things. She knew that the saltiness of the olives would ensure that they kept drinking the frothy cocktail. "Good man," remarked Peter. "I won't send him to the dungeon for daring to make a decision for the king. And the queen..."

He poured a drink for each of them and lifted his glass to touch hers. Peter turned very serious, "Be sure to look into my eyes when you toast," he said. Lauren was puzzled. "If you don't, it's seven years of bad sex." Lauren stared at him intently as she raised her glass.

Dinner began with an appetizer platter of chilled seafood that they shared, followed by grilled marlin caught that afternoon. The margaritas kept flowing. Somehow, despite all the food and the drinks, Lauren and Peter still ordered dessert, a decadent concoction of bitter chocolate and orange sorbet. By the time the waiter cleared the table for the last time, the garden was in complete darkness, save for the perforated paper bags holding tea light candles to outline the paths. It was enchanting. The ambiance worked its magic on Lauren and Peter. If they were nervous when they arrived, they left the restaurant arm in arm, like the lovers they knew they would become.

Peter walked Lauren home through the darkened streets. As they approached the villa, he told her quite plainly that he wanted to spend the night. This time, his directness did not take her by surprise. Throughout their rambling conversation during dinner, Lauren realized that being completely straightforward was a feature of Peter's personality. He did not play word games.

Peter had not hesitated to tell her that he was married and the father of two teenagers. But in his view, it was perfectly logical and possible to be attracted to her and still love his wife. He was on vacation in many ways. He had spotted Lauren walking on the beach from the balcony of his hotel room and watched her for several moments before tearing out to catch up to her. There was something about the way she walked that intrigued him. Peter could not explain the attraction any better than that. Lauren understood completely. Wasn't she still incapable of describing what had drawn her to Richard?

Why did it feel so different, now that she was the single one and the man was married? Perhaps because Lauren was not betraying anyone by sleeping with Peter. She was no longer married and in an odd way, the fact that Peter was, made it easier to be with him. Lauren knew from the outset that this would be a brief romance. She felt safe in knowing the precise boundaries of this relationship. She was not ready for a deep emotional entanglement, but she did admit to herself that she missed sex.

Peter was a gentle and thoughtful lover. He undressed Lauren slowly and deliberately, exploring each part of her body as he exposed her skin to the night air. Lauren lay in the huge mahogany bed, with the overhead fan turning lazily and the cool night breeze wafting through the open shutters, as Peter covered her skin with kisses that raised goose bumps on her belly and limbs. He pulled the sheet over her briefly while he stripped off his clothes, keeping eye contact with her all the while.

With the taste of chocolate and oranges still on their tongues, Peter and Lauren kissed long and deeply. Peter covered her body with his, then began kissing her chin, then her neck, working his way to her chest, stopping to circle her breasts and nipples before continuing on to repeat the circles at her navel. He gazed up at her before continuing his tour down her body.

Lauren ran her fingers through Peter's hair, then grasped his back and massaged her way down his spine, stopping only when her arms could reach no further. She grabbed the headboard to steady herself. When she thought she could not hold on much longer, Lauren nudged Peter onto his back. She turned over and straddled him, gasping as she took him into her body. Her hands on Peter's shoulders, she moved rhythmically, staring into his eyes until they both shuddered from the release that followed. Lauren collapsed onto Peter's chest and lay there, trying to catch her breath. The pounding of Peter's heart, only inches away, reverberated in her ear.

"Thank you," whispered Peter when Lauren rolled off him and covered them both with the sheet.

When the rooster crowed the next morning, Lauren was confused to find that Peter was not in bed. Grabbing her robe, she walked out to the terrace to find Peter soaking in the plunge pool. Thankfully, Lauren had told Peter about Maria. She was glad that his boxer shorts could pass for swim trunks. Lauren handed Peter a towel to wrap around his waist. Together, they strolled to the dining area to enjoy breakfast. The omniscient Maria had prepared two glasses of orange juice and had set the table with coffee and fresh fruit and toast for two. Bless her.

Peter had only two more days in Puerto Vallarta. He asked Lauren if he could stay with her until he left and she agreed without hesitation. He checked out of his hotel and brought his bags to the villa. They spent the balance of their time together in quiet companionship. They wasted no time talking about the future. What little time left was all they had and somehow that made it easier to enjoy each other. When they spoke, it was about intangibles, about theories of life and dreams both fulfilled and otherwise. They adopted an unspoken rule not to discuss anything concrete, like dates and times and places.

They made love. In the morning, spurred on by the rooster. During the day, when Maria disappeared after her chores. In the evening, after dining at another local restaurant, hurrying through the meal to get back to the villa again. Peter and Lauren were like kids at an amusement park. They knew that the good times would end soon and they focused on enjoying the ride rather than bemoaning how little time remained for them to share.

On his last afternoon, Peter packed to leave. They agreed that Lauren would not go to the airport with him. She was relieved that she would not have to return to the villa alone. When it was time for him to go, Peter kissed her and embraced her tightly, then turned and left in the waiting cab. That night, when Lauren turned down the bed, she discovered a note on her pillow. 'Thank you,' he had written. He enclosed his business card, with his personal email address hand-written on the back. Lauren smiled at the name he used: PeterPan2 certainly captured his approach to life. She was not sure what to do with the card. She tucked it into her cosmetics bag where it would be safe but out of sight.

The rest of her escape in Mexico passed in a haze. Peter was on her mind as a pleasant memory; she did not consider him a heartache. She tried not to think about how he would describe his stay in Puerto Vallarta when he returned home, then chastised herself for being concerned with something she would never know more about. Lauren was proud of herself for taking a chance with Peter. She truly had enjoyed the wonderful interlude with this sensitive kiwi. It was so good to be with someone who made her feel special again.

Lauren returned to Chicago to find a note from a florist on her door. A delivery had been left with her next-door neighbors. She dumped her bags in the vestibule, then knocked on their door. Gina and Tina (Lauren called them the Na-na sisters) welcomed her back before handing her a flower box. The Na-nas insisted that she open it immediately. Inside, Lauren found a dozen exquisite long-stem roses. The bottom of the box held a card from Peter: 'Don't forget me.'

Refusing to answer any questions about the sender, Lauren rushed home. After putting the roses in water, she unpacked, experiencing a pang of emotion when she found Peter's business card in her make-up bag. Not knowing what to say about the flowers, Lauren sent him a quick email saying, 'I don't know what to say. Except that I couldn't possibly forget you.'

How would she ever be able to explain the Peter story to her women's dinner group? They met for dinner from time to time to bring each other up to date on the events in their very diverse lives and to talk about all and sundry. They had been meeting now for almost 20 years and there was very little they did not share.

Larger than the women's group that Lauren so enjoyed in Boston, they were the Chicago six: Jeanine, Deirdre, Caroline, Melanie, Hélène, and Lauren herself. They tried to coordinate their schedules to meet, although frequently at least one of them had a conflict and was unable to attend. It seemed that more and more, they were all so much busier.

What was interesting about the women was how interconnected they were. Lauren had met Jeanine when they were colleagues at the APRA and they remained friends even after Lauren no longer worked there full-time. They had supported each other through their very different marital crises and sympathized when their children acted out in the most outrageous ways.

Deirdre was a childhood friend of Lauren's. They were in elementary school together in San Francisco, then lost touch for many years. Once they reconnected, quite by accident, they became fast friends again. Deirdre worked with Caroline at the Museum of Science and Industry.

The two remaining women were Melanie and Hélène. Melanie was a friend of Jeanine's. They had met at a Pilates class. Hélène knew both Deirdre and Caroline; they were all in the same theater club. It was somewhat surprising that in a city as large as Chicago there was such overlap in the women's friendships. On the other hand, each of the women was part of several other large circles of professional and social contacts. Although they saw each other occasionally at other events, there was something special about the six women that kept them meeting as a group for so many years.

They had been through pregnancies, divorces, illnesses and deaths, affairs and romances (there was a difference), changing careers, fluctuating finances, and new homes. They had celebrated major birthdays together, calmed each other when their kids pushed their buttons, congratulated each other when these same children married, and dutifully oohed and aahed over baby pictures of new grandchildren. In short, they tried to be supportive of each other and they succeeded more often than not.

When they first began to meet, Hélène felt it important for them to have a name. Although they met only in the evenings, they agreed on 'The Ladies Who Don't Lunch' because it clarified who they were not as well as who they were. Like Lauren, all the other women worked. Some needed to, others wanted to, and some worked for both reasons. They didn't have time for lunches, but enjoyed spending the occasional evening with a group of like-minded women who could – and did – talk about just about anything.

When the Who Don'ts – that was their nickname · arrived for dinner at Lauren's shortly after her return from Mexico, the roses were still on display. It took about three minutes for the interrogation to begin. 'Who sent them?' was the universal question. Lauren laughed; three minutes was a long time. She poured sangria for the women and began the story of Peter and La Casa de la Mujere. She continued the tale through dinner, providing more details as the women questioned her between bites of the Mexican dish she had prepared: chicken with bitter chocolate sauce. As was the custom, the Who Don'ts brought dessert. They enjoyed the sweet pineapple and plump grapes as they sipped their coffees.

"So what are you going to do about Peter?" asked Jeanine.

"I really don't know," Lauren replied quickly. "The whole thing was so unexpected and so wonderful. But I really thought it was over when Peter left Mexico and I do not know what to do about a married man who lives in New Zealand and sends me roses. What can I do?"

Several of the women spoke at once. "Go see him," said Deirdre. "Yes, that's a wonderful idea," agreed Melanie, who had never married.

"No it's not. It's absolutely wrong," countered Caroline, who had been married forever.

"I'm not sure you should do anything until he answers your email," Hélène advised.

Caroline jumped in again. "What do you want to do?" She was a romantic at heart.

"I really can't answer that. As I said, it was all so unexpected. And coming so soon after my divorce, I am not used to being in such predicaments. Although I must admit it was definitely a change from bedtime with Richard."

The women laughed, sipped their coffee and fell silent for a moment. It seemed appropriate to end the evening at that time. The women found their coats and stood for a moment at the door. "Keep us posted," reminded Melanie.

"Stay tuned." Lauren waved goodnight to her friends. She realized after they left that they had forgotten about the charitable aspect of their dinners. "Too bad. But we can make up for it next time," she announced to the empty room.

Lauren blew out the candles and cleared the table. She loaded the dishwasher and washed the pots, stemware and salad bowl. Funny how she was becoming such a creature of habit. She caught herself mumbling, "This goes here. And this goes here.

And this goes here," as she put away the dinner things. "I'm becoming an eccentric old woman," she whispered. And she began to cry. Tears streamed down her cheeks and she sobbed miserably.

Lauren sat down in the darkened living room and poured the last of the sangria into her glass. She wondered where her outburst had come from. She stared at the roses and she knew.

When Lauren had found herself alone after her separation from Richard, she was miserable. It was the shock of being one person by herself, when she had been one of two, then three, then four as her family grew. She had not realized how much she would miss the background noise of other people. She had not expected to ache at the loss of even casual physical contact. There was no-one to talk to as she puttered around the kitchen or the garden. There was nobody to touch her hand or inadvertently bump against her as they went by. There was no-one, period.

Of course, she spent time with colleagues, clients, and friends, especially the Who Don'ts. And she did see the children when they came home for holidays and breaks. But increasingly, Emma and Jason became just a little bit less familiar each time they reunited. They were becoming their own people and Lauren was glad for that and proud of them. But at the same time, they were leaving less space for her in their lives.

It had been the same for Lauren when she went to Berkeley. Even though she was not close to her mother, she loved her parents and often thought about them when she was at school. On her trips back to San Francisco, she always found time to visit her parents in their separate homes. But eventually she began spending time with her friends at their family homes or at resorts catering to the university crowd, where no-one expected her to be their little child again. Now the next generation was treating her the same way. Perhaps it was inevitable.

She sometimes wondered whether Emma and Jason were also losing their closeness to Richard. Lauren's connection to him was sporadic, at best. There was little reason for them to communicate, except to talk about the children. Increasingly, that conversation was about financial obligations. When they first separated, Lauren occasionally sent Richard an email about her family's news, but after he remarried, she stopped. She realized how far the ripple effect of their divorce had spread when Richard's niece married and Lauren found out from her children only after the fact. The girl had been all of two years old when Lauren came into her life and Lauren was her only aunt. They had lost touch abruptly when Lauren and Richard separated.

Was it fair to expect that they could continue a relationship? Lauren knew that it sometimes happened. Hélène kept up at least cordial relationships with some ex-family members. Even after her ex-husband remarried, she remained on good terms with her former mother-in-law. There was no guidebook for these things and once again, Lauren wondered about all the relationships lost when she and Richard divorced.

So why was she upset about this thought now? Lauren had cried and cried when she first separated from Richard. Then, after her aha moment about choices, she trained herself to reframe her circumstances and to at least look for the joy in every situation. That was one of the reasons that she so embraced her escape to La Casa de la Mujere and her affair with Peter.

The problem was, neither of those extremes of emotion was reality. Elation was just as unreal as despondency. Now that she was back from her holidays, it was time to moderate her emotions and recognize that life was not really a rollercoaster ride. It was more like a superhighway and she was speeding along without really knowing how or when she would reach her destination. She sighed, flashing back to a time many years earlier, when Emma was a baby. Lauren and Richard had met another young couple at the park one Sunday afternoon. While the men stood pushing the babies in the little swings, the two women sat chatting on a bench. They discussed how difficult it was to raise their kids without grandparents and extended family nearby.

Lauren commented on how odd it was to have no destination for their weekend outings. "We're all looking for our destinations," commented the other woman sagely. Lauren looked at her in surprise. The remark was much more profound than the conversation warranted. "Oh, sorry," said the other woman with a laugh when she saw Lauren's expression. "I'm going through analysis now as part of my psychiatric training. Seems I can't say anything mundane anymore."

Lauren tried to normalize her routines. She made a conscious effort to focus on the projects at hand, but to leave work at work at the end of the day. Using a home office made that a challenge. For one thing, she could work in her bathrobe in the middle of the night if she wanted to, as long as she made her deadlines and was available for client meetings.

Lauren decided to make herself her first priority. She began working with a personal trainer, having sessions with him twice a week and going to the neighborhood gym on other days. She bought a yoga video and did the routine several times a week. She watched what she ate. As the pounds fell off and she toned up, Emma and Jason began to notice a difference in her. The children warned her that she was becoming a hot mama. Lauren was delighted.

During one of their visits to the house in Hyde Park, Lauren talked to Emma and Jason about selling the family home. She had given up so many other things in the divorce settlement to keep the house, so that the children would have some place familiar to come home to. Even then, she had to pay out Richard for his share. Now, the house was no longer important. It was too big for her and she did not want the responsibility of taking care of it on her own. Much to her surprise, the kids were very supportive about her moving. They told her that they were too adult to sleep in their childhood bedrooms anyway, which made Lauren smile. They often found very special ways of helping her out.

Lauren decided to put the house on the market. At the same time, she began to look for a condominium on the North Shore. It took forever to go through the big house, clearing things out and making it more presentable. Where was it written that as the mother, she was the one to keep all the kids' memorabilia, from preschool artwork through high school trophies? She tried to get Jason and Emma to go through their things on their next visit, but all they succeeded in doing was creating new piles for her to store. Her new apartment would have to include a locker.

It took six months for Lauren to get the house into shape for selling. It was an emotional rollercoaster clearing out over twenty years of accumulated stuff. The process was supposed to be cleansing emotionally, and that was true to an extent, even if it sometimes felt that the cleaning agent was either abrasive or caustic or both. Lauren was surprised at how few things she still owned that predated Richard. She remembered collections of owls and shelves of books by her favorite authors, but could not find them anywhere. Presumably, she had given them away years ago, but it disturbed her that there was little evidence of her full and productive life before her marriage.

Lauren was also surprised at the number of items she found that belonged to Richard. She thought she had cleared the house of everything that was his. What was she supposed to do with photographs of him as a child? Yes, the children might like them, but Lauren felt that they were Richard's to dispose of. And what about a fly-fishing rod that had sat, unnoticed, in the garage? And a pair of his cufflinks that she discovered at the bottom of one of her old evening bags?

She sent an email to Richard, asking if he would like these things. His response threw her. He did not want to give her his address and asked, instead, that she have the children give him his things the next time they saw him.

Lauren refused. Really, they were still the parents of two children, even if the children were young adults. They should always have each other's contact information, if only for emergencies. Lauren wrote back. She explained that she wanted his address and cell phone number, in case she needed to reach him if something urgent came up, especially with the children. She asked for the same courtesy from him. Finally, he relented. Men! How could she have married someone so thick?

Never mind. She really had no desire to stalk him – Lauren just wanted to get rid of his things. She boxed them all up and sent them to Richard the next day. She included all the cookbooks with his handwritten notes scribbled in the margins. He certainly was a good cook...

The house did not stay on the market long and Lauren sold for what she considered a good price. She used the proceeds from the sale to purchase an apartment in one of the newer buildings along the lake, just north of the Loop. She was relieved that she could buy without taking out a mortgage.

The days of packing seemed endless. Checking her email late one night, she found a note from Peter with an unexpected invitation. Lauren was surprised to hear from him. There had been occasional emails and even phone calls from time to time, but with all the details involved with selling the house and buying her condominium, she had pushed Peter out of her mind. Unable to decide how to respond, Lauren chose to sleep on his request. The next morning, another dozen roses arrived. This time, the card read, 'Please say yes' and was signed, 'From the man who asked you out to dinner.'

Lauren put the roses into a bottle she retrieved from the recycling bin. They looked ridiculous jammed into the neck of the plastic container, but it would have to do. Vases, like everything else, were packed in one of the growing mountain of boxes labeled 'Fragile & Heavy.' She was not going to unpack until after the move. Lauren put the flowers beside her laptop and wrote a quick response to Peter. 'Dear Mr. Roses, Dinner at my new place. I will order pizza. Wear jeans and be prepared to help me move furniture.'

The day of the move, exhausted from the many trips between her old and new homes, Lauren took a quick shower in her new bathroom and put on a clean sweater and a fresh pair of jeans. She let her curly hair air dry because she could not find the dryer. And she made do with only the lipstick she kept in her purse, for the same reason. She had not thought to put cosmetics into her 'Open Me First' suitcase of fresh clothes and linens for her bed. She hoped Peter would be too jet lagged to look too closely.

Lauren unpacked a corkscrew and unearthed a bottle of wine. She opened another box containing kitchen ware and set the dining room table for two. She did not have the time to look for a vase.

She was in the midst of setting up her CD player when Peter arrived. She showed him in and he immediately enveloped her in a tight embrace, followed by a lingering kiss. When they pulled apart, Lauren gave Peter a quick tour, skirting the boxes and unwrapped furnishings so that they could admire the view out over the lake. When Peter noticed the juice container holding the flowers, he quipped, "Good thing I brought you this." He handed Lauren a housewarming gift. It was a beautiful hammered silver vase and Lauren put it to use immediately.

The pizza arrived and Lauren and Peter enjoyed their meal. After two glasses of wine, Peter struggled to keep his eyes open. The combined effect of jet lag and the alcohol did him in. He apologized for his behavior and looked at Lauren questioningly. "I'll call a cab for you," she said. And the moment was lost.

Peter phoned her when he got back to his hotel. "I'm so sorry I fell asleep. Please let me see you again, Lauren." He sounded quite wide awake. "I promise not to conk out on you if you let me take you out to dinner tomorrow."

The next night, they ate at the top of the Hancock Building. Lauren had progressed far enough in her unpacking to retrieve a silk knit dress to wear, along with heels and a cashmere wrap. Peter had never seen her wearing anything this citified. They were a long way from Puerto Vallarta.

Dinner and dancing rekindled the romance they had experienced in Mexico. Peter took Lauren home and once again told her directly that he wanted to spend the night. Lauren knew that there was only a very short period before Peter left for more business meetings on the east coast. Still, she was unsure how she felt about inaugurating her new apartment with Peter. It was a silly sense of superstition, not wanting her new bed to be his. She invited Peter in for a while but insisted that he return to his hotel for the night. She explained that she was unsure how to handle his sudden reappearance. He was not happy about her decision, but left when he once again had trouble staying awake.

The next day, they agreed to see each other after Peter's last meeting of the afternoon. They visited the Art Institute and walked through Millennium Park and along Lake Michigan, side by side but not touching. That was what bothered Lauren. She did not feel honest being in public with a married man. Even though there was very little likelihood that anyone who knew Peter would see them, Lauren worried that someone who recognized her would ask about this man.

Back at her apartment once again, Lauren explained her perspective to Peter. "Yes, I really enjoy being with you," she admitted, happily. "But it isn't right; it goes against my sense of fairness to continue a relationship with a married man. It is not fair to your wife; it is not fair to me; and it is not fair to you, either." Peter countered that it had been heavenly being together in Mexico. "Yes, I agree. But that was the fantasy of the villa. This is reality."

Peter continued, "It's wonderful being with you. And it doesn't take anything away from my marriage."

Lauren could not accept that. She took a deep breath and tried to speak softly rather than angrily. "Please don't say that. I do not even like hearing that sort of rationalization from you. Peter, what you are doing – what we are doing – is not right. I'm not saying you forced me into anything. I got involved willingly and eagerly, that is true. But I certainly did not expect it to go this far. I thought that when we parted in Mexico, that was the end."

Peter continued to try to explain his viewpoint. "When my wife and I were first married, we went to a gathering where another man came onto her very strongly. It was such a turn-on for me. It is the heightened sense of attraction that I get. That time, it was because someone else was making passes at my wife. This time, it is because I am so attracted to you. It's what turns me on."

Lauren did not see the analogy. She knew that it would be easy to take Peter to her new bed and that sex with him would be wonderful, again. But the attraction was not as strong as in Mexico. True, she still felt the pull of his voice and his particular way of speaking. And Peter did look wonderful this evening in his business suit. Perhaps that was the problem though. This was no longer a sabbatical or vacation in Mexico. Lauren was now back to the business of her life in Chicago. And she did not want that to include sleeping with a married man who would be leaving her, again, the next day.

She rose from the couch and took Peter's hands. She pulled him to his feet and looked up into his eyes. "You can't stay, Peter. I'm glad we saw each other again, but you are flying out tomorrow and I wouldn't feel good having you stay with me only to leave again." He looked at her determined face and took her hand, walking towards the door.

"OK, Lauren, I'll go." He kissed her quickly on the cheek as he had when they met at the restaurant in Mexico. Then he left.

Much to her surprise, after living in the large house in Hyde Park for so many years, Lauren acclimatized to her new home with ease. She jokingly referred to the smaller space as her reduced circumstances.

Her condominium contained a decent sized master bedroom, a large living room with a gas fireplace and a smaller second bedroom that she used as a combined home office and den. The kitchen was much smaller than the one in her old house, but it had a great view out over the lake that expanded her horizon. The only drawback was the lack of outdoor space. The owners shared the rooftop deck and some of her neighbors did a little gardening up there, but it was not the same as having a huge backyard and Lauren would miss her patio, too.

Lauren had downsized dramatically in terms of furniture when she moved. She sold and gave away not just the pieces from the children's rooms, but also many of the things from her marriage to Richard. Her new home was an opportunity to start again. How often did that happen? It did not mean that everything must be new, but Lauren was determined that her condo would contain nothing with bad karma for her. Only positive energy, please.

Lauren wanted her new home to reflect her new view of herself. She no longer needed to use practical fabrics and materials that could live up to the demands of her family. No teens would stretch out on the couches and no pajama parties would take place on the living room rug. Lauren was glad that there would be no more pop spilled and she secretly hoped that future spills would be wine - spilled in the heat of passion, perhaps. "What a vivid imagination I have," she said to herself, enjoying her silliness.

"Perhaps I should ask Neil to help me with the décor," she continued. Neil was a gay neighbor who had given her a tour of his apartment, commenting on the appropriateness of each piece of furniture for some romantic or sexual position. "Perhaps not. I didn't worry about the furnishings at the villa, and that did not seem to matter…"

She hoped that the condominium would be her home for a long time and she wanted it to have a good foundation, so Lauren did not stint on the furniture that she really wanted. Her first purchase was new bedroom furniture to replace the pieces she and Richard had lived with for so long. Then, she continued from room to room, building around the pieces she had held onto from the house; some had belonged to her even before meeting Richard and she could not part with them. The result was eclectic, but she was proud of the outcome. She filled her apartment with a mix of monochromatic contemporary pieces offset by the occasional splash of color, whimsical accent, or antique piece that she just could not part with. She surrounded herself with the potential of new things, balanced by the familiarity of the old.

Once the furniture was in place, she experimented with her art, moving it around the condominium several times before finally deciding where to hang the framed pieces and to display the sculpture. She knew that she would continue to add artwork that called out 'Buy me!' in local galleries and on her travels. She could always find room for one more piece to display. Rearranging artwork was one way to refresh the apartment from time to time, even though it meant more and more holes in the walls.

When everything was more or less in place, Lauren sat down to admire her handiwork. She poured herself a glass of wine, turned on some music and lit the fireplace. She toasted herself. "I am starting something new in my life here and I want it to be a wonderful new chapter. Here's to new chapters and here's to me, even if I have no-one's eyes to look into at the moment."

The phone rang, interrupting her thoughts. Lauren picked up, to hear a cheery 'Hello' from Brenda, a friend from high school who still lived in San Francisco. Brenda very unexpectedly became pregnant in 10th grade. When she told her family, they all but disowned her, insisting she was a bad influence on her younger siblings. They would not let her continue to live at home. The school also made her leave, despite the fact that Brenda was an honor student. With no education to speak of, and no family to support her, Brenda became a mother at 16.

Lauren admired her friend's ability to deal with whatever was thrown at her. Despite all the nay-sayers who predicted otherwise, Brenda did marry the child's father, who supported her through the pregnancy and encouraged her to continue her schooling. Brenda is still married to him. She really defied the odds. Brenda completed high school through correspondence courses, then went on to college and graduate school. She and her husband had two more sons. Lauren admired her tremendously and was always glad to hear from her.

The timelines of their lives were so out of sync. Brenda was already a grandmother by the time Lauren was pregnant with Jason. When they talked, the two friends often compared their lives. Brenda felt that she grew up along with her children; when they went off to college, she joined them. By the time she turned 40, she was free of the day-to-day obligations of parenting. She pursued a career in early childhood education and because of her age and maturity, moved quickly up the ranks in the Montessori system.

Lauren, on the other hand, had a good start on her career before she married and had her kids. When she gave birth to Emma, her hospital room mate was exactly half her age. Whose life was better planned? With a 20-year commitment to each child, Lauren and Brenda debated whether it was better to have a family sooner or later. There was no right answer.

Brenda was planning to attend an upcoming conference in Chicago on early childhood education and attention deficit disorder. "Could I stay with you?" she asked. Not only did Lauren agree, but she decided to speed up her plans for an open house, so that Brenda could attend. It would be a chance for one of her oldest friends to meet some of her newer ones.

The housewarming party was on a blustery fall night. The wind howled off the lake. The fireplace was a welcoming feature as her guests arrived, shivering from the cold. As requested, many of her friends brought champagne. Others brought housewarming gifts, despite Lauren's instructions to the contrary in the email invitation. Still, she enjoyed the special presents, always surprised at how well some of her friends knew just what she would like. Unfortunately, not all her friends shared this talent; Lauren would regift the things some people brought. "What a wonderful word," she muttered to no-one in particular as she unwrapped something from the Na-nas - a kitchen counter ceramic recycling bin decorated with worms and bugs. Lauren knew the moment she saw it that she would donate it the local resale shop supporting street kids. She hoped the sisters would not ask her about composting.

The Ladies Who Don't Lunch arrived en masse, making the party an even more special event. Deirdre was glad to see Brenda again and enjoyed introducing the other Who Don'ts to her. Together, they regaled them with tales of Lauren's high school escapades in San Francisco. Lauren overheard the first story, describing a serious crush she had on the captain of the debating team and the weekend they broke into his parents' house in the mountains. She left them all laughing uproariously, amused that these old stories still raised eyebrows. Did her friends think that her high school behavior did not mesh with her as a grown woman?

In addition to the Who Don'ts, Lauren's guests included a few colleagues from work, as well as friends from Hyde Park and her neighbors from the adjacent apartments. She wanted to win them over, rather than risk their potential complaints about the noise and the use of so many spaces in the guest parking area. Initially, she worried that the women would outnumber the men. She dismissed her concern when she realized that there were some things even she could not control.

Many years had passed since Lauren last entertained on her own. She was nervous about having so many people over without Richard as co-host. To help the evening run more smoothly, Lauren handed out assignment cards to some of her guests. Because Brenda was staying with her, Lauren asked her to answer the intercom and buzz people in. Hélène was responsible for taking coats. The other Who Don'ts worked to keep the hors d'ouevres plates filled, passing the food to the other guests. One of her neighbors volunteered to take over opening the champagne after Lauren almost broke a ceiling light fixture when she popped the first bottle. The small jobs served as ice-breakers as the guests joked about how Lauren organized them so that she could be a guest at her own party.

Lauren was happy to see her new home filled with the people who mattered to her. At first, she was sad that Emma and Jason were not able to come home for the weekend to attend. But after her third glass of champagne, she forgot that small disappointment. She served as tour guide repeatedly, realizing how proud she was of the way she had decorated her apartment with the things that were most important to her. Lauren liked looking around at the people enjoying themselves in her new surroundings. "I hope my home always welcomes people who care about me and vice versa," she whispered. "And I am glad that Brenda is the first person to sleep over, rather than Peter."

Neil arrived with his partner, interrupting Lauren in the middle of her thoughts. Together, the men presented Lauren with a magnificent orchid plant in a beautiful Chinese porcelain planter. It was stunning in its simplicity. Lauren was touched. She hoped that the beautiful gift would survive in her care, an unlikely event given her record of either under- or over-watering every plant she had ever owned. She made a mental note to read up on orchids, hoping that the plant would thrive in her new home. That would be a good omen.

Several bottles of champagne later, the guests began to leave. By midnight, Lauren found herself alone with Brenda. They rehashed the evening, with Lauren enjoying Brenda's perspective on the Chicago crowd. "They all adore you," Brenda insisted. "They think you walk on water. What did you do to make them think that?"

Lauren laughed at the comment. "They are all good friends, it's true. Of course, I have known the Ladies Who Don't Lunch for almost as long as I have lived in Chicago. And my APRA colleagues have become more than just work friends. But you know, when Richard and I split up, many of our friends disappeared."

"How's that?"

"It's weird, really." Lauren took another sip of champagne and thought for a moment before continuing. "There was a group of people, mostly couples, who formed a movie club that met the third Wednesday of every month. Nothing formal - we took turns picking a film and sending out an email with the details. Whoever showed up, showed up. It was mostly couples, but not entirely so. There were some single women and even some single men."

"Sounds like fun."

"It was. And after Richard and I split, I went to the films a few times. At first, people seemed not to know what to say to me. It was as if I had the plague. It's funny, because before, we would all just sit beside each other without making a big deal of it. We would meet about 20 minutes before the film and if we were in a conversation with someone, we would just sit down next to him or her when the film started. Boy, did that change."

"How so?"

"What happened was that all of a sudden, I guess I was seen as a threat. There was one couple in particular that I always suspected had a shaky marriage. The husband was a real flirt. You know the type; he thought he was God's gift to women, although I cannot imagine why. When he did pay attention to his wife, it was as if he was showing off his devotion. I always suspected that he cheated on her."

"Don't tell me he came on to you."

"No, he didn't. Or if he did, I was too dense to realize that." Lauren paused to choose her words. "But what happened was that when I started attending the films alone, he became extremely formal with me. And every time he started to talk to me, his wife would come and join us. It was as if they were both on high alert with me. Him, because I think he knew I suspected him of cheating on his wife. And her, because I think she was afraid that I would be his next conquest. It was so uncomfortable that I stopped going after a few months."

"Did you ever see Richard there?"
"No, thank heavens. I really did not want to run into him. I know he went a few times, but we never were there together. Perhaps

it was awkward for him, too. I really don't know. And now that I've left Hyde Park, I may never go again, so it's really a moot point whether Richard shows up."

Brenda looked at her friend for a while. "Did you ever regret the break-up with Richard?"

"Not for a nanosecond. Of course, I would have preferred if our marriage had survived. But I've told you what happened. It is true, you know. The warning bells that I ignored at the beginning of our relationship were the very alarms that signaled the end."

"Don't you just hate it when those platitudes turn out to be true?"

"You know, when Richard and I split, I swore that if one more person told me to take baby steps, or to choose another street, or to live one day at a time, I would knock them upside the head. It was infuriating to hear all that sugar-coated advice and I thought I was above all that. But after a while, I realized these corny expressions have some truth to them. That's the thing about generalities, you know. They are generally true. Now I find myself telling other people the same platitudes when they are having rough times."

The two women laughed, each lost in their own memories of trauma and stress they had come through. "God only gives you what you can handle," Brenda intoned in a preachy voice.

"Arghhh! I hate that expression! Or at least, I used to. I thought it was a real catch-22. What choice did I have but to handle all the things thrown my way? What choice did you have but to raise a child when you were little more than a child yourself?"

Brenda sat quietly. They rarely spoke about her early pregnancy. She looked at Lauren when she replied, "I always hated it when people told me how capable I was and how I would always land on my feet."

Lauren nodded in agreement. "I know what you mean."

"But recently, I've come to realize that being capable and always landing on my feet are real gifts. And I am proud of my abilities. You should be too, Lauren."

They sat for a while in the darkened living room, staring out beyond the windows at the blackness that was the lake. After a while, they cleared the glasses and dishes, loaded the dishwasher and got ready for bed.

In her bathrobe, Lauren knocked on the door of the den, where Brenda was sleeping on the sofa bed. "Thanks for being here with me, Brenda. There's something so wonderful about having you here, such an old friend, witnessing me as I start my next big adventure."

Brenda opened her arms to embrace her. "What are friends for?" Lauren sat on the edge of the bed and the two women hugged.

After Brenda's visit, Lauren settled into a comfortable routine. She renegotiated her contract with the APRA to include spending at least one day a week at the corporate headquarters. While she enjoyed working out of her home, she also missed the collegiality of the office. She enjoyed going back to hear the latest office politics as well as the most recent in-house developments in her field. One of the reasons that Lauren still enjoyed working for the APRA was the sincere effort it made to be responsive to real patients and their advocacy groups. Another was the organization's on-going education for staff of all levels.

Lauren had left the corporate offices of the APRA as Senior Executive Vice President, an impressive title that included 60-hour weeks and far too much travel. When the children were young, she felt she had to find a way to spend more time with them. The APRA agreed to Lauren's suggestion that she become a consultant to the organization and after brief negotiations on the details, they reached a mutually satisfactory arrangement.

Lauren had been on retainer with the organization ever since. She was responsible for one long-term project – putting out a quarterly journal for hospital and nursing home executives across the country. Its goal was to remind the readers repeatedly not to forget the patients in their quest for better bottom lines. It was an uphill struggle. Still, the publication she produced was well-respected in health care literature and Lauren had received several awards for it on behalf of the APRA.

Publishing the journal developed a rhythm of its own. Lauren was constantly searching for authors. Encouraging health care executives to write was an ongoing source of angst. With each edition, Lauren worried that there would not be enough quality material to receive the approval of the peer-review editorial group. "It's like pushing a rope," Lauren would say when asked how she convinced people to submit manuscripts. And that was just the beginning.

Lauren found that she needed to do more than just encourage these executives to write for her. Their writing skills were not their strong suits. And that was the diplomatic explanation. Lauren remembered one author who wrote, 'We must be broad-minded and focused.' She was still trying to figure out how to accomplish that without crossing her eyes. Another author talked about 'unlocking the key.' He was not referring to a second level of security.

Working on the journal took perhaps a third of Lauren's time, although as deadlines drew closer, she still worked long days. Each time she published a new issue, however, Lauren felt that she had once again created something special and valuable. There was tremendous satisfaction in holding a copy in her hands and she looked forward to the Letters to the Editor that always followed.

The best part of the contract with the APRA was that, other than the journal, there was no requirement for Lauren to do any other work. As a contractor on retainer, Lauren was paid whether or not there were projects for her to oversee. It did not happen often, but occasionally, when the career gods were with her,

Lauren would have a period when she put the journal to bed for another quarter and there was no other project for her. Imagine being paid for not working.

Over the years, Lauren had learned that her boss had a soft heart exceedingly well-hidden under a very prim and proper exterior. Alan Forester was one of the few men who still wore three-piece suits and wing tip shoes. He had recruited Lauren to Chicago many years earlier and had mentored her throughout her rise in the organization. Somewhere along the way, they developed an easy understanding of each other as both corporate and private individuals. But Lauren didn't let on to the other staff that she knew Alan as anything other than his very conservative self.

The State of North Dakota wanted the input of the APRA on rationalization of hospital and nursing homes. They were about to review inpatient services across the northern part of the state and were concerned that patients might be unhappy if they suggested amalgamating some facilities and closing down others. "No surprises there," Lauren remarked when she met with Alan for an initial discussion on the project. "The real question is, do they want the APRA onside to make it appear that they care about the patients or do they really want us to help organize patient input?"

Alan sat across from her at the small round table in the corner of his office. "Just like you, Lauren, to cut to the chase. Why don't we wait and see?" They had gone down this road before and each knew how the other felt about groups that involved the APRA to put a better spin on unpopular decisions. "We'll head up there next week for a couple of days and see how we can help."

Lauren was not exactly eager to head to snow country in the middle of winter, but travelling for projects was part of her arrangement with the APRA. It seemed to her that she was always going to wintery places in February or March. "I guess I'll have to dig out my woolies again," she laughed.

"I wouldn't know about that. I'm sure by now you know how to pack," Alan said, looking at her very seriously.

Lauren and Alan met at O'Hare on Sunday. The flight, via Salt Lake City, got them into Butte late that night. It was the only way to be ready for the Monday morning meeting with officials of the state hospital and nursing home associations. Alan and Lauren barely spoke during the trip. Even away from the office, Alan was not good at small talk. Lauren remembered many years earlier, taking a flight with Alan to visit the New England Regional Office. When she asked him about his two young children, Alan was not sure what grades they were in at school. It cut further conversation very short.

The meeting with the officials went well. Alan agreed to have the APRA coordinate telephone polling and face-to-face interviews with individual patients and advocacy groups across the affected counties. Lauren would coordinate the project, working with local hospitals and nursing homes to ensure patient privacy and anonymity. It was always a challenge to ask people for their opinions when their records were confidential.

When the meeting concluded, the rest of the project team unexpectedly invited Lauren and Alan on a visit to some of the smaller communities that might be affected by the mergers. They could hardly refuse, even though it meant extending their trip. They rented a van, equipped with snow tires and chains, to navigate the snow-covered roads. Before they left, Lauren checked that the vehicle also had an emergency kit of a shovel, flares, candles, matches and solar blankets. She insisted that they purchase bottled water and dehydrated food. Alan knew better than to remark on Lauren's emergency preparedness routine. She had once driven off the road in the back country of Utah. It had taken more than 16 hours for the Sherriff's Department to find her, huddled in her car. Ever since then, Lauren always registered her vehicle license number and personal information with the Department of Highways before heading out in winter in remote areas.

They left on their tour the next day and reached the first small town by noon, in time to visit the local 13-bed hospital and sample its catering for lunch. It would be very difficult for the small community to lose this facility. Asking the locals to go elsewhere for care would be like asking someone in Chicago to drive 200 miles to another hospital. Lauren was prepared to hear about the difficulty of driving in winter to the next facility, even though it might be only fifty miles away. What was the conversion factor for one northern snow-covered back country mile to a big-city throughway mile cleared as soon as the snow fell?

The project team intended to visit another community that afternoon. They set out again, with Alan driving. The snow fell harder and harder, to near white-out conditions. The caravan slowed down almost to a standstill. Cell phones did not work in the mountainous area; Alan flashed the car's headlights repeatedly to signal to the others to pull over. When the drivers huddled at the side of the road to discuss their poor progress, even the locals admitted they were not comfortable driving in such weather. As darkness came early at this time of year, they agreed to stop at the next motel to spend the night.

The motel was a scene from a grade B movie. It was nothing more than a group of wooden cabins set very close to the edge of the highway. Alan left Lauren huddled in the car and went to inquire about vacancies. There were only three rooms left. One was a dormitory, with four bunk beds and a bathroom down the hall. Two were single rooms hardly larger than closets. As the only woman in the group, Lauren claimed one of them. Alan took the other. The rest of the team would have to bunk together.

The snow almost blinded Lauren when she carried her suitcase into her little room. She was very glad she had worn high shearling boots and a long down-filled, hooded coat. She and Alan agreed to meet the rest of the group for something to eat at a diner down the road, before the storm made driving impossible. During the meal, there was little small talk as the team repeatedly glanced out the window at the worsening storm. This kind of weather made her very nervous. Lauren was thankful that they made it back to the motel without incident.

She undressed and changed into her nightgown, wrapping herself in the blanket from the bed to keep warm. The room was very draughty and the single-pane window rattled in the wind. She sat down to watch the one channel available on the ancient television. A few moments later, someone knocked on the door.

Lauren grabbed her coat and put it on over her nightgown. She opened the door a crack, unwilling to let snow blow into her room. There stood Alan. "Would you like to come next door for a nightcap?" he asked, sheepishly. He was looking Lauren up and down, not knowing what to make of her outfit. Her bare feet showed below the hem of her long coat and her bare throat peaked out at the neck.

Lauren realized how strange her get-up was, but she was cold and she had not been expecting company. "No thanks," she replied, perhaps a little too abruptly. "I'll see you in the morning."

She closed the door before Alan could say anything else. The door to her room did not lock properly. In the movies, someone always jammed a chair under the door handle to keep out unwanted guests and Lauren copied the move. She tossed and turned in the single bed beneath the window before finally falling into a light sleep. Some time before dawn, someone pounded on the door. Lauren awoke with a start. If the intruder pushed hard enough, the door would open and he would be in bed with Lauren. "Hey buddy, get your ass out here," shouted the man who stood just inches away from Lauren outside the cabin.

"There's no-one here but me," Lauren managed to reply. The banging on the door stopped and Lauren peaked from behind the curtains to see a construction worker moving down the row of cabins, knocking on doors as he went. When the group assembled for breakfast, they guessed that the construction crew had had too much to drink the night before. It was little solace to Lauren. "Whatever the excuse," Lauren mumbled, "I thought that I might have someone in bed with me if I wasn't careful." Alan looked at her strangely when she made that comment.

Thankfully, the rest of the trip was uneventful. The storm passed and the group was able to visit other facilities before Lauren and Alan returned to Chicago. Lauren arrived back at her condominium late at night. It was the first time she had been away from this home. She left her suitcase in the vestibule. She hung her bulky winter coat in the closet, took off her boots and changed into a robe and slippers.

She poured some single malt scotch into a crystal tumbler and added a drop of water. She turned on the fireplace and put on some music. Unpacking could wait. The mail could wait. It was good to be home.

Every time she went north, Lauren wondered whether it was such a good idea to be so good at her work. Each time she traveled, the positive working relationships she developed with the locals resulted in another invitation to return. It was a vicious circle. Of course, the visits always took place in winter. Lauren had been caught in snow storms as early as September and as late as June. Summer was not a predictably reliable season in North Dakota.

This was to be her last trip on the regionalization project. By now, people in the small communities throughout upstate North Dakota recognized Lauren. The municipal politicians and employees pitched the virtues of their communities, staging coffee meetings with local service clubs and advocacy groups to bolster the case for their local facilities to remain open. The institutional executives and physicians, who feared for their local facilities, briefed their staffs well. And of course, most of the patients praised the facilities as if they were the Mayo Clinic. Everyone realized that some small hospitals and nursing homes faced closure, but no-one wanted the closure in their community.

Lauren did not enjoy being the bearer of bad news, but she knew that when she wrote the report, she would recommend transferring patients with serious conditions to bigger, better-equipped facilities. She would not want to have surgery in some of the small hospitals, where colored tape on the floor marked the sterile field outside the operating room. The locals thought otherwise.

After a long day of listening to one more group extol the virtues of their wood-framed, 38-bed hospital, Lauren drove to the local motel. The rationalization project was so political that she had to stay at inns on the highway, rather than favoring one community over another with her presence. It was ridiculous, really. She checked into another Bates Motel look-alike and found her room at the end of a long corridor. The dining room was closed. Dinner would be a protein bar and bottled water.

Lauren opened the closet to hang up her coat. Inside, she found a pair of men's pants dangling forlornly from a hook. She was more than a little surprised. She called the front desk to report the lost clothing. "Did you check the pockets?" was the response from the night desk clerk. Lauren chose not to examine the trousers.

She climbed into bed without checking the sheets either. She had to trust that germs could not survive in this frigid weather. Lauren watched the local news while munching on her protein bar, then turned out the light. The bed was lumpy, but she was tired from the day of driving and smiling and listening. She realized how the APRA faced the dilemma of recommending something that patients would not appreciate, even though it would result in better care. It was a very familiar scenario. And it was the type of decision that Lauren was paid to make.

Lauren fell asleep with the television still on. She awoke about an hour later, when the channel went off the air. She felt a stabbing pain in her lower back that she attributed to the poor mattress. But as the pain increased, Lauren recognized the symptoms as the beginning of a kidney attack. This was the first one since she had left Boston. When she could no longer pretend that the agony would go away, Lauren called the front desk. She was certain she woke the night clerk.

"I'm Lauren Saunders in 112."

"Yes, I know who you are." Lauren was not sure that was a good sign.

"I need a doctor. I'm having an attack of pyelonephritis and I need help."

"Pile-o-what?" came the response.

"Never mind. Just get a doctor on the phone and I'll explain," Lauren gasped as another wave of pain came over her. She hung up and doubled over.

A few moments later, the phone rang. Lauren explained the problem to the physician. Because the emergency room at the nearest hospital was closed for the night, he agreed to come to the motel as soon as possible. That turned out to be 40 minutes, which only served to remind Lauren how difficult it was not to have immediate access to medical care.

The young doctor arrived and brushed the snow off his parka when Lauren let him into her room. She recognized him as one of the members of the medical staff that Lauren had interviewed earlier in the day. Lauren recalled that he had been particularly vocal about the need to keep the small hospital open. He was professional enough not to say anything, but Lauren sensed that this visit was not going to be fun.

The doctor listened to Lauren relate her symptoms, then gave her a cursory examination. The local pharmacy was also closed, leaving only one solution to relieve Lauren's pain. The doctor had her lie on her stomach and hike up her nightgown. Perhaps it was the pain she was in, but Lauren was convinced that the young doctor took particular delight in plunging the syringe into her exposed backside.

He left Lauren with a prescription for antibiotics and more pain killers. He also recommended that she cut short her trip and return to Chicago, suggesting that she would be more comfortable getting further medical attention there. Lauren thought she detected some sarcasm in his voice when he talked about proper medical care. But she was too dozy from the effects of the pain killer to do anything other than thank him and promptly fall asleep. He let himself out.

In the morning, still sore and disoriented from the narcotic injection, Lauren called Alan and told him about the attack. He immediately took charge, arranging with the car rental company to pick her up and take her directly to the local airport. She knew she was too woozy to drive. All she wanted to do was sleep, in her own bed. Besides, the gossip about the APRA consultant's come-uppance would be all over the region by now and Lauren did not really want to face it.

By nightfall, she was back in Chicago. On the way into town from O'Hare, she checked her voicemail and found a message from Alan. He had pulled strings to arrange an appointment for her with the Head of Nephrology at Northside Hospital the next day.

Oddly enough for someone who advocated for patients' rights, Lauren disliked hospitals. "They're full of sick people," she muttered as she walked down the corridor of Northside Hospital, painted predictable hospital green. "And they smell funny." It was not a great attitude to have but it was with her as she waited to see Dr. Rognon. How could a physician with that name have chosen any other specialty?

Dr. Rognon was younger than Lauren was. "Are medical schools accepting students directly from kindergarten?" Lauren's inner voice asked as the physician introduced herself. Lauren shook her hand and then showed her the prescriptions from the northern doctor.

Dr. Rognon glanced at them, then returned them to Lauren. "I understand from Alan Forester's frantic call that you have a history of kidney infections. When did they begin?"

Lauren related the tale of her first attack, when she was living in Boston some 30 years earlier. The nephrologist there was at least twice Kay Rognon's age. He prescribed a course of antibiotics to treat the first attack. When Lauren returned to his office two weeks later, she complained that the problem had returned. The older nephrologist argued with her that a recurrence was impossible, given the course of drugs she had taken. Lauren argued back. "I took the drugs exactly as prescribed. And all I can say is that once again, it hurts like hell."

"The condition simply cannot have returned this quickly. The pain must be in your head," he intoned.

Lauren was furious. "I don't care where it is. All I know is that it's as painful as it was fourteen days ago." The doctor was not impressed with Lauren's outburst. He wrote her a prescription for valium.

It was Lauren's first experience with tranquilizers. She took the first dose before bed, as prescribed. A few hours later, she had a frightening hallucination. Not knowing whether she was awake or asleep, Lauren saw large, feral dogs circling her bed. She screamed and scrambled for the bedside phone. Her first instinct was to call Michael, her boyfriend at the time. Fortunately, he was a physician and his apartment was in the same complex as Lauren's.

It didn't take long for Michael to arrive at Lauren's. When he saw the prescription, he was livid. The dosage was enough medication to tranquilize a 250-pound man. Michael thought Lauren should sue for malpractice. She was happy just to fall asleep with Michael sitting beside her on the bed. She felt safe with him there. But the episode turned her off tranquilizers. She never took them again, always listing valium when asked about drug allergies.

"No wonder you had that look on your face when you walked in," Dr. Rognon remarked when Lauren finished. "I couldn't tell if you were angry or terrified. I guess it's a bit of both." She had a very matter-of-fact tone and spoke without belittling Lauren. I will send you for some tests to be certain, but I am confident that this recurrence was a random reaction to the stress and the cold of snow country. Alan told me where you were when the attack came on. I really do not think it is anything for concern. The shot you received probably hurt your pride as much as anything else did, but you did receive the right treatment and the proper dosage for the prescriptions from the local doctor. I know him; we went to medical school together." She smiled as she handed Lauren a requisition for an abdominal ultrasound. "If you don't hear from me within two days of the test, it means everything is fine."

The Who Don'ts had not convened in a while. Lauren contacted them all, declaring it was time to eat. The emails flew back and forth, as the women tried to accommodate everyone's schedule without planning so far in advance that by the time the date arrived, someone would have to cancel because a conflict arose in the interim. Caroline ultimately made an executive decision and invited the group to her home. She lived in a big house in Hyde Park, not that different from Lauren's previous home.

The night that The Ladies Who Don't came over, Caroline's husband disappeared. Although most of the women had met him, he was a complete mystery to Hélène, who had not. She insisted that he was a figment of Caroline's imagination. Caroline and Dave had been married for almost 30 years. Their parents had played bridge together for years; the couples were such good friends that their children's romance was almost incestuous. They had been high school sweethearts who never dated anyone else and everyone just assumed that they would marry one day.

Still, Caroline and Dave delayed their wedding until after college. They both went away to school in Michigan and came home to Chicago together for all the holidays. Three weeks after receiving their degrees, they were married. Dave went on to graduate school in Chicago, becoming an economist. He chose an academic career and ultimately had tenure at Illinois Lakeside College. Caroline ran her father's fitness equipment business, applying her marketing skills to bring the family company into the 20th and then the 21st centuries. Their plan was for Caroline to work until their first child was born.

Caroline and Dave learned the meaning of the expression about always making plans in pencil. After trying to get pregnant for three years – that would be 36 periods arriving to deflate their hopes – Caroline and Dave sought help. They went through countless tests and procedures to determine if there was a medical reason for their infertility. There wasn't.

"Try harder," said the doctors.

"Relax, you're trying too hard," advised their parents.

"Try more often," laughed their friends.

After much soul searching, they decided against in vitro fertilization. They both desperately wanted a child, but they were concerned about the mental toll the procedure would have on them. They did not have any success adopting.

They kept trying the old-fashioned way, as Caroline put it, until one day they just made love for each other, with no thoughts of calendars or timing. Of course, that is when Caroline conceived. She was ecstatic, as was Dave. Their parents, who no longer knew how to talk to them or each other about the lack of a grandchild, were over the moon. Caroline and Dave were only children and bore the additional burden of having to continue the generations of the two close families.

Her pregnancy went beautifully. There was no morning sickness and Caroline truly blossomed as the months passed. At eight months, she recruited a new general manager for the family business. She was not planning to go back to work. Four days before her due date, she went into labor. Her water broke as she and Dave were putting the finishing touches on the nursery. Caroline's bag was packed and they drove the short distance to the University Birthing Center relatively calmly.

While Dave filled out another round of paperwork, Caroline was greeted and escorted to the birthing room. When Dave joined her, Caroline was in full labor. The baby they had dreamed of for so long was now in a hurry to arrive. The obstetrical nurse examined Caroline then quickly left the room. Dave continued to help Caroline breathe. He was too busy to notice the look of concern on the nurse's face.

A moment later, the obstetrician arrived. She was not Caroline's doctor, who was still on his way to the Center. "The baby is transverse - lying across your abdomen. We are going to try to turn him." Before Caroline could say anything, a nurse attached a line from an IV bag to the port on the back of Caroline's hand and tightened a mask over Caroline's face. Caroline was alert enough to turn on her side when asked to do so. Another doctor who had slipped in behind Caroline began to administer a spinal anesthetic. Everyone was talking very quickly, getting consent from Dave before ushering him out of the room.

The doctor worked to turn the baby, finally delivering a healthy girl by cesarean section. She was cleaned up and put into a bassinet while the obstetrician prepared to deliver the placenta. As the doctor began, Caroline went into medical distress. Her heart rate plummeted and the anesthetist was unable to bring her blood pressure back to a safe level. The nurse called a Code Blue and within seconds, a team sprinted into the room pushing a crash cart ahead of them. The team worked on Caroline for about ten minutes to regulate her vital signs. When Dave was finally allowed back into the room, he found his wife looking very pale and frightened. Caroline was stable again and her incision had been closed.

The nurse turned to the bassinet to hand the baby to her father. Only then did she discover that the infant had turned blue and was barely breathing. In the rush to save the mother, the newborn was left unheeded for a moment too long. Deprived of oxygen, she had suffered irreversible brain damage.

Their beautiful baby girl looked perfectly healthy. But she was not. Pediatric neurologists conducted days of tests but the results were unequivocal. Their daughter, whom they named Zara, had lost most of her brain function and had no chance of ever breathing on her own. She could live for many years in an institution, but she would never recognize her parents and she would never even know she was alive.

Caroline and Dave held their infant daughter in their arms, talking to her, crying, and praying. They asked her to forgive them for the decision they made. They bravely smiled at Zara, holding her as the machinery helping her breathe was unplugged. They held her until she turned cold in their arms. Then they wept some more.

Years passed and Caroline and Dave relived the tragedy repeatedly when they sued the hospital for negligence. All they wanted was an apology. They never got one. Ultimately, the hospital settled out of court, offering money but never admitting culpability.

Despite the tragedy of losing Zara, Caroline and Dave grew stronger as a couple. After a time, Caroline used some of the settlement funds to go back to graduate school to study fundraising management, which led to her job at the Museum of

Science and Industry. Dave moved up the academic ladder, travelling extensively to lecture around the world. They drew strength from their love, their extended families and their faith. Caroline encouraged Dave to have a vasectomy and they kept their family as just the two of them.

When the Ladies Who Don't Lunch first began meeting, Caroline introduced a charitable element to their dinners. The process was simple and had worked for years. The hostess chose a charity and the Who Don'ts each contributed $10 to the cause. Over the years, they had donated thousands of dollars to a wide variety of groups that benefited from an additional $60 or so. This time, Caroline chose to donate funds to a small not-for-profit that paired university students with high school students from the inner city. The mentors helped the younger kids with homework assignments and took them to classes on campus several times each term to pique their interest in post-secondary education.

The charity was the brainchild of young man who was an associate professor in the Faculty of Education at the University. He had grown up in the projects and would not have completed high school without the encouragement and persistence of his basketball coach, who recognized the potential of the young student. They both realized that the chances of avoiding gangs and drugs and actually completing secondary school were remote without hands-on guidance. The older man sat with the boy every day after practice, helping with homework. After initially resisting, the teen found his academic stride and not only completed high school, but also won a scholarship to Lake Michigan University. He continued his studies until he obtained a doctorate, writing his dissertation on the role of mentorship as a retention method to help keep inner city children in school.

His little charity was his way of giving back. He coordinated all the partnerships himself, recruiting university students from across the campus and meeting with local school principals to identify students who might benefit from the mentors. It was a lot of work, in addition to his own teaching and research, but it meant a great deal to him. And he knew how much it could help. The small donation from the Who Don'ts would cover some of his out-of-pocket expenses and provide a few more high school students with proper school supplies, too.

With the charitable recipient of the dinner selected, Caroline chose a topic for dinner discussion. With so many dinner discussions behind them, the women knew each other's backgrounds. Still, they always spent a few moments catching up on the latest news. Then, rather than allowing the conversation to drift, Caroline asked the women to discuss acts of charity. "What is it that makes people give to others, whether money or time?"

The discussion was lively. Some of the women talked about their charitable budgets and how these had changed over the years. Not surprisingly, many of them had donated to feminist causes when they were younger and some still did. Others gave significant donations to charities dealing with children, especially when their own were young. Some were going back to those charities now that they had grandchildren. Hélène, who had been diagnosed with breast cancer five years earlier, still supported the cure. Melanie, whose father had died of ALS, had that charity high on her list.

What was the correct amount to give? No-one believed in formal tithing, but a consensus developed. Give until it hurts. Or better said, give until you feel it. Otherwise, it is not charity; it is just pocket change. Deirdre was employed in communications and public relations at the Museum; her department and Caroline's worked closely together. She picked up on the theme of how much to give. "There are always kids panhandling outside the Museum. They stand just off the grounds on public property, running to squeegee the windows of cars stopped at the light at the exit. People give them money all the time. But I don't. They frighten me and they annoy me at the same time."

Jeanine jumped in. "I always give them something because I hope someone would do the same if it were my kid standing there."

"That's an interesting perspective," interjected Caroline. "A generational variation of 'there but for the grace of God go I,' I suppose." She paused. "At the Museum, fundraising is an ongoing challenge. People question if we are still relevant, given the instant availability of all kinds of information on the Internet. I get tired of justifying our existence."

Deirdre spoke again. "It's interesting that people continue to think of museums as the same vintage as the relics on display. To many people, we provide entertainment. Our visitors don't realize how much they are learning when they tour the exhibits. And because they think we are all fun and games, they think that donating money to us is somehow frivolous. After all, with so many serious issues such as poverty and inadequate education and homelessness and addictions and I could go on and on, how can we even think of asking for money for a museum? It's really frustrating."

Caroline stood up to bring coffee and tea to the table. "Don't let me stop you all," she said. But dessert distracted them and the conversation on charity wound down. "Let me just remind you,"

Caroline said when she poured coffee refills for the group, "that so far all we've talked about is the financial aspect of giving. Maybe next time, we can go beyond our wallets. Speaking of which, get out your ten-dollar bills and ante up. It is $20 each this time. We forgot all about charity when we met last time at Lauren's."

The women put down their money on the table, then pulled out agendas, blackberries, and smartphones to find a date for their next dinner. It would be Jeanine's turn next.

With encouragement from Emma and Jason, Lauren began dating again and was slowly developing a relationship with a man she had met on-line. Even she was surprised that she registered a profile at brainiacs.com. It was a website for more mature people who had something between their ears besides cotton batten. More mature translated into over 45. Her friends warned Lauren that the first rule of Internet dating sites was to lie about her age. She felt that was a strange way to begin a trusting and honest relationship, so she told the truth.

Lauren signed up with the dating website not really knowing what to expect. With her password, she was able to review hundreds of profiles of men in and around Chicago. She felt like a kid in a sexual candy store as she began to read their stories. They sounded too good to be true or too off-the-wall to even contemplate. It did not take long for her to make her first decision, to eliminate anyone who did not post a photo. Either they were too awful to look at or they were not computer-savvy enough to upload a shot from a digital camera. She did not want to risk either scenario.

Some of the photos she saw amazed her. Many men posted shots that included their pets. Others showed themselves posing with babies (grandchildren?), young women (daughters?) and not-so-young women (ex-wives?). What was most surprising was how poorly groomed some of them were. Lauren remembered a comment her mother often made, 'Remember, that's what they consider their best photo. You can just imagine...'

The photos of unkempt men showing off their beer bellies or sporting hair pieces that did not fool anyone were a real turn-off. Lauren was not looking for perfection, but she did want someone who rated at least a 6.5 on a scale of one to ten for appearance and grooming. Comb-overs would never make the grade.

The first man she met misled her by posting a photo that must have been 15 years old. In the shot, he looked like a successful entrepreneur, with broad funky suspenders showing over a white shirt he wore with the sleeves rolled up. They emailed a few times, then arranged to talk on the phone. Because she was not comfortable giving out her home phone number, Lauren was careful enough to be the one to call, using her mobile phone. Their conversation was fast-paced and all over the map.

The man spoke about himself in new-age terminology, which did not sit all that well with Lauren. But she was determined to give him the benefit of the doubt. He claimed to be a writer of pop-psych books and was in the process of preparing his next manuscript. "I'll send you a link to the draft," he volunteered. "Let me know what you think."

Lauren thought that he was a very poor writer and that Alan Forester would accuse her of purple prose if she ever wrote anything like that in one of her reports. She was beginning to regret agreeing to meet him for coffee. She hoped he would forget to ask her opinion. He didn't forget and Lauren had to deflect the questions about his work with vague suggestions and comments.

They met at two o'clock the following Saturday. He had told her in advance that he had only 90 minutes, as he planned his days very carefully and did not like to deviate from his schedule. That should have been enough of a warning, but Lauren was curious, and they were meeting in a public place in the middle of the day. She thought nothing could go wrong.

Again, she thought wrong. The man who walked up to Lauren was at least 30 pounds heavier and was much balder than she expected. He looked like the father of the man in the photo. He was covered in dog hair, which he explained by launching into a long story about his two brats. Lauren finally asked him who they were. "Why, my dogs, of course."

This was going to be a very long hour and a half. The man liked the sound of his own voice. He told Lauren several of his pop-psych theories of life, none of which made any sense to her. And then he told her point blank what he was looking for in a partner. "Short term, I would like a woman who will spend Wednesday evenings and Saturday mornings with me. Those are my free times at the moment. I turned my day around to accommodate this afternoon coffee break with you, Lauren."

"Oh," was all she could say.

"And long term, I want someone who will take care of me when I am older and become sick or disabled. Of course, if you are the one who needs care, I will be able to look after you. I know how. One of my dogs died a few years ago and I nursed her for a long time before I had her put down."

"Yes, I see," came out of Lauren's mouth.

"Well, even though I have a few moments left, I'll leave you now. I feel that this relationship won't progress very far because

I can tell you aren't a dog lover," he said with considerable disdain.

Lauren hadn't thought she was that transparent.

"But I want you to know that I'm OK with that. Because when I'm faced with a situation that I don't like, do you know what I do?"

"I can't imagine."

"I ask myself what JC would do."

Lauren thought that Jesus should tell him never to contact her again and she prayed for that message to get through. The man looked at the bill, calculated his portion, put some money on the table and left. Lauren just shook her head and watched him climb into his car. His two large dogs were pawing at the windows as he drove away.

Undeterred, Lauren continued corresponding with other men on the brainiacs site. She hoped that her first experience with Internet dating was going to be her worst. It did not have to be her last.

The next man she met was an architect. This was not a good idea from the start, as Lauren feared he would remind her too much of her ex-husband Richard. Worse, they might know each other. They met for an early dinner on one of the days that Lauren worked at the APRA offices. He was late arriving because he had to pick up one of his sons from school. And he could only stay so long because he had to be sure the kids did their homework and went to bed at a reasonable time.

Was this what happens to men who divorce the mother of their children to marry a much younger woman? Why are they surprised when the younger woman wants her own family? The architect had left his second wife only a year ago and had joint custody of their two adolescents. From his first marriage, he had grandkids not much younger than these two. Much though she loved children, Lauren had no interest in having to plan her relationship around a man's kids. She was not good at sharing that way.

She left the dinner disappointed from learning about his family obligations, but decided that she would see him again if he asked. A few days later, she received an email from him saying that he had not felt any chemistry and while she was nice... Lauren was furious. And insulted. She wrote him back that she did not believe chemistry was instantaneous and that she could not recall the last time she had made love on a restaurant table. She never received a reply.

Over the next few months, Lauren met several more men through the brainiacs site. She drank more cups of coffee and sipped more glasses of wine than were good for her health. And most times she came away disappointed. The few times that she wanted to see the man again, he didn't call. Lauren was still too old-fashioned to be the one to initiate a second meeting.

And then she met Thomas (always Thomas and never Tom or Tommy). He was a civil engineer who conducted research for a company developing macro-level energy-efficient forms of inner city transportation. On their first date, Lauren and Thomas walked from the Hancock Building, where they had met, to the Wrigley Building and back again. Along the way, Thomas talked about a concept he was working on to use electric cars to reduce dependency on gasoline. He explained how parking meters would be re-engineered to boost cars that needed more energy and to drain their energy for street lighting when the cars sat idle. Parking stalls in garages would have similar outlets, providing energy when the car was turned on and draining it from parked cars to light and heat the buildings above. In his system, energy was not stored in the vehicles, but drawn on when needed. It was fascinating. And the best part about the conversation, to Lauren, was that Thomas just assumed she understood everything he was saying.

Perhaps there was something to the name of the website service after all. Smart was indeed sexy.

Thomas and Lauren began to see each other on a regular, if not frequent, basis, because he was always busy. Lauren joked that Thomas elevated being busy to an art form. If he was not behind on deadlines at work, he was giving tours of his lab to visitors from other jurisdictions. If he was finally finished a grant proposal, he was preparing a chapter for his next book or a monograph for a journal. And if somehow, miraculously, he had cleared his calendar, it was usually because he was about to travel to some world capital to consult with the locals about applying energy conservation to public transportation.

How he ever found time to see Lauren was a mystery, but he did. Lauren teased Thomas about being so busy but she rarely said no when he asked her out. She liked his company enough not to play hard to get.

They enjoyed the theatre and opera together, with Lauren occasionally inviting Thomas to use one of her season's tickets seats. They ate at obscure ethnic restaurants throughout the city; Thomas had an unending list of good places to eat. Their evenings always ended at Lauren's. Thomas would come up for a nightcap that became two, then three. He had the ability to consume copious amounts of alcohol seemingly without any side effects. Lauren did not even try to keep up. After their first date and late drinks, Lauren insisted that Thomas take cabs to and from her apartment. She was terrified that he would be involved in an accident if he drove.

Thomas was about ten years older than Lauren was. Still, he was fit and healthy and, most importantly, incredibly smart. Lauren thought his brain was his sexiest feature. This turned out to be truer than she would have liked. The first time they made love, Lauren discovered Thomas' limitations in the bedroom. It was not that he was poorly endowed; quite the contrary. The problem was that he could not get an erection. This was a new situation for Lauren, who was discreet enough not to say anything to him about her disappointing discovery.

Thomas seemed unperturbed by his lack of performance. He said their bodies had to get used to each other. But as time passed and they spent more nights together, nothing changed. They tried various positions, props and toys, without success. Thomas seemed not to notice that something was missing. He was attentive to Lauren and frequently brought her to orgasm in other ways. Still, she tired of the gymnastics that sometimes helped Thomas position himself better, and to her surprise, she missed the more mundane positions that had worked for so many for so long.

She talked to Hélène about her situation and was not comforted when her friend told her she had experienced the same thing. "It's what happens to lots of older men. To be terribly crude, they cannot get it up any more. And if they can, it does not stay up. C'est la vie.

"Most men are too proud to ask their doctors for Viagra or Cialis. And the ones who do ask are the ones who do not really need it in the first place. They use the drugs to enhance their erections. It's absurd. I mean, what woman wants to be with a man who has a 4-hour erection? Honestly! If only doctors would give prescriptions for Viagra or Cialis to the women, it would make everyone's life easier."

Lauren laughed. "Hmmm, do you think this could be a new cause for the APRA? Should I raise it at the next executive meeting? I can just imagine the look on Alan's face."

Bedroom disappointments notwithstanding, Lauren enjoyed her times with Thomas. She found him incredibly sexy, even if he was not very good in bed. It felt odd for her to be judging a man's sexual prowess. It had never really occurred to her before that she had preferences in the bedroom.

Thomas broke his pattern of claiming to be busy, inviting Lauren to his home for dinner on her birthday. He came to pick her up and walked into the living room while Lauren retrieved her coat. Earlier that day, another dozen roses had arrived from Peter. They were displayed in the silver vase Peter had given Lauren as a housewarming gift.

"Did I send those?" Thomas remarked, a little confused.

Lauren blanked for a second. Then she clarified, "They're from an old friend. He always sends me roses on my birthday." She did not want to say any more. Although she loved the flowers, she did not like having to explain them. The next day, Lauren sent an email to Peter thanking him for the most recent bouquet and requesting that it be the last.

Jeanine's birthday fell a month after Lauren's. The first of the Who Don'ts to turn 60, Jeanine planned a special event to share with her friends. She convened the women, asking them to promise not to give her the bumps. As usual, the other Who Don'ts agreed to bring dessert. They opted for a decadent chocolate extravaganza as a birthday cake and ordered it large enough to accommodate many candles. The women also decided to bring champagne to toast the birthday girl.

Jeanine was an elegant looking woman who dressed more like a New Yorker than a mid-westerner. Her clothes and jewelry were always tailored, but far from staid. Jeanine was a very tall woman who still weighed what she had in college. The other Who Don'ts were not so fortunate and were definitely envious. Despite her lithe body, Jeanine did not flaunt her figure. Her signature approach to fashion was that she always wore black. And her jewelry was always silver. The contrast against her caramel skin and white hair was striking.

The night of the dinner, Jeanine glowed. The Who Don'ts had treated her to a spa day for her birthday. She had been so relaxed after the pampering that she had to nap before her friends arrived. As a surprise, Jeanine had hired caterers for the dinner. "It's my party," she sang to the tune of an old song, "and I'll splurge if I want to..."

Jeanine handed each woman a different flute for the champagne. As monochromatic as she was in her dress, she had a very eclectic collection of stemware, cutlery and china. The Who Don'ts always enjoyed the look of the table at her house. No two place settings were the same and each had a story. Jeanine was a collector and kept notes on where, when and how she acquired each piece.

The first course was a hearty soup of roasted vegetables. While the caterers served, Jeanine steered the conversation to the theme of the evening. "I wanted to use the subject of birthdays because they are the one day in the year when it's socially acceptable to be self-centered and self-indulgent. And as the senior member of the group, I feel the responsibility to prepare you all for the days that you, too, reach 60." The women laughed; it was not like Jeanine to be immodest.

"Some of us still have a way to go, you know," Melanie interjected. She was the youngest in the group.

"Don't remind me. Seriously, though, there is something about turning 60 that I think is quite different."

Caroline interrupted. "I thought 60 was the new 50."

"That may be, but how many of us were excited to turn 50? My point is, as young as I might feel, I have to admit that I am definitely no longer middle-aged."

"And so what do you plan to do about that?" Lauren asked.

"Well, I have two announcements that might answer your question. First, I've decided to take early retirement from the APRA."

The women were all shocked, but none more so than Lauren. She was gob smacked, to use an expression her mother-in-law had taught her. She and Jeanine had met at work and had become friends in and out of the office. As Vice President, Member Services, Jeanine's job entailed working very closely with the regional offices and state and local chapters of the organization. The two women often worked together on projects and Lauren would miss her friend's availability as a sounding board and her contributions as a colleague.

"Retired? Then what?" asked Caroline.

"My second announcement is that I've decided to leave Chicago, at least for a while. I want to spend some time working in a developing country, while I still have the stamina to do so."

The Who Don'ts stopped eating. While the caterers cleared the soup plates and served the main course, the women all seemed very intent on studying the china and crystal in front of them.

"Ladies," Jeanine said to change the mood at the table, "I am not going to become a recluse and I'm not taking vows of either poverty or silence. I am just going to get involved with a marvelous charitable organization that I want you all to donate to this evening. It works in emerging countries to raise the standard of education for young girls. You know that's something I've always cared about."

"Jeanine, it's not that we're not happy for you. It's just that we'll miss you," Hélène offered. "And we can't imagine a dinner without you here. Perhaps we could consider this your sabbatical from the Ladies Who Don't Lunch. All in favor?"

All the women raised their hands, with Jeanine's the highest. "Well, that settles that," she said. "I'm relieved that you won't disown me. Now, let's finish the main course so that we can move on to dessert. I can't wait to see how we fit all those candles on the cake."

The conversation flowed more easily, once the shock of Jeanine's two announcements wore off a little. There were many questions about the charity, the countries where Jeanine might be posted and what she might end up doing. Jeanine answered their questions as best she could. She impressed her friends with the single-mindedness of her decision.

Lauren wondered about the timing of it all. She decided to speak to Jeanine privately for more details. That weekend, they got together for brunch.

Jeanine talked almost non-stop about her decisions. Now that her mind was made up, she was truly committed to this new course of action. As she spoke about her plan to retire early and to work in a developing country, she became more and more excited. Retirement and volunteering were linked in her mind to a new stage of life. She wanted to take care of herself and pursue interests that required donating more than a few hours a week or even a week or two of vacation time. The only way to accomplish this was not to work full-time any more.

Jeanine was a widow; ten years earlier, her husband had died of pancreatic cancer just short of his 53rd birthday. His death followed a year of increasingly desperate searches for a cure. Towards the end, Henry endured the testing and procedures more for Jeanine than for himself. He knew he was dying and had little time left, but Jeanine could not and would not accept this. They were a devoted couple and it was brutal for Jeanine even to imagine life without him.

Their children, both in their late teens when their father died, could not console their mother. Certainly, she was incapable of comforting them. Jeanine fell into a deep depression after Henry passed away and took months to come out of it. That was when she rid her closet of anything that was not black.

The Ladies Who Don't Lunch spent as much time as possible with Jeanine when she was in mourning. They brought meals, organized counseling for the children and even hired a part-time housekeeper for a few months. They accompanied Jeanine to grief support groups and took her for walks and drives. They worked out a schedule of visits to ensure Jeanine was not alone in the evenings. Sometimes, they came over just to sit in the same room as her, brewing and serving endless pots of tea that Jeanine barely touched. Often, they held her as she sobbed.

When Jeanine was strong enough to return to work, she relied on Lauren for emotional support during the day as well. Lauren's office became Jeanine's haven when she lost focus and needed a place to regain her sense of equilibrium. They became even closer friends and confidantes. She stayed with her job at the APRA after her husband's death because she needed the security of something familiar in her life.

While Henry's estate was not large, his insurance did give Jeanine a financial cushion that could support a more than modest lifestyle. Prudent investments had increased her savings. Now, despite the fact that her pension would be smaller than anticipated because of her early retirement, she could afford to stop working and still live quite comfortably without eroding her capital too significantly. Her children were adults with children of their own. It was time for Jeanine to move on.

Lauren was envious, but realized it was bizarre to be jealous of a woman who went through what Jeanine had. Certainly, the grief she experienced after her separation from Richard did not compare to Jeanine's when Henry died. What Lauren admired was that Jeanine had somehow developed the strength to move on in her life. It had taken a long time, but Lauren had witnessed the changes in her friend's frame of mind and the gradual improvements to her self-confidence.

Lauren smiled at Jeanine warmly as they enjoyed another cup of coffee. "I'm proud of you, my friend. You have finally become unstuck. You know my theory about implosions and you've proved it."

Jeanine had heard this before but in the past it had never rung completely true. "I finally understand. When Henry got sick, I could not believe this was happening. It was not just his life that was cut short, I felt it was mine, too. You know how I dragged him hither and yon, looking for someone or something that could help."

"Don't do this to yourself, Jeanine. You did what you did because you loved him. Focus on that."

"Thanks for saying that, but I did what I did for me, mostly. It took years of therapy for me to realize that. I practically abandoned my kids, you know. Thank heavens for you and the other Who Don'ts. I do not know how I would have coped without you all looking out for them and me. You really went beyond the call, you know."

"Jeanine, we did what we did because we wanted to. My point is that when your world imploded, you were stuck for a long time. Now, look at you. You are about to take off on your next big adventure. I am so proud of you. I'm envious, too."

"Well, I admit it's taken me a long time to get past Henry's death. As you would say, I will never get over it. But I am past the heavy grieving now. Not quite ready to give up black, but who knows what will happen when I'm posted to sub-Saharan Africa."

Lauren looked at her friend, who was always so elegant. She tried to picture her in 100 degree heat, dressed in her usual way. She suspected color would come into Jeanine's life in many ways, but she kept that thought to herself. Jeanine was making a huge change in her life. Lauren wondered whether she would ever have the courage to do something so drastic.

The annual conference of the APRA was a three-day event, bringing together organization representatives from the regional, state and local levels, members of the public, medical and professional staff and institutional management executives. It also attracted policy makers and politicians from federal and state governments who, in turn, ensured widespread media coverage.

Lauren and Jeanine were heavily involved in putting together the conference schedule, which included plenary sessions, workshops, and panels. These days, they left the arrangements for logistics and social events to the company hired to stage the event. The planning for the meeting almost never stopped, with suggestions for the following year culled from participant evaluations and the occasional note that Lauren, Jeanine and their colleagues scribbled on the ubiquitous conference notepads when something went particularly well – or off the tracks.

With her imminent retirement, this would be the last conference that Jeanine attended. Lauren wanted to arrange a farewell event of some kind. Alan agreed to host a surprise luncheon in her honor, inviting the heads of the regional offices and state chapters and others who had worked closely with Jeanine over the years.

Jeanine called Lauren when an email from Alan Forester announced a schedule change. "Did you see it? I wonder why. We always have lunch with John Bell-Kingsley on the Thursday before the AGM. Now I'll have to change my flight to get back to Chicago later, given that this will be my last command performance."

Lauren kept mum on the reason behind the rescheduling. It was hard to keep a secret from Jeanine, especially with so much going on in the last days before the conference. "Well, I guess tradition is about to be changed. Besides, staying another few hours in San Diego is not such a hardship. In fact, I am planning to stay overnight on Friday, heading back the next day. Want to join me?"

"No thanks," Jeanine replied. "I always find the conferences so exhausting that all I want is my own bed as soon as possible. I'll still be able to get back to Chicago on Friday, even if it will be the middle of the night." They left it at that.

The executive staff of the APRA flew down to the venue early in the week of the conference. There were always one-on-one meetings before the official opening session on Wednesday morning. And once the conference started, it was like running a marathon. As Jeanine arrived for lunch on the Thursday, Lauren caught up to her at the entrance of the coffee shop. "Alan left me a voicemail saying that he's changed the venue. He has arranged room service in one of the seminar venues so that we have room to work. Let's go." They headed for the stairs to the conference level floor.

When she pulled open the doors and saw all the people seated at tables set for a meal, Jeanine looked questioningly at Lauren. Before Jeanine could say anything, Lauren gently pushed her into the room and everyone stood to applaud. When Alan Forester greeted her from the head table, Jeanine finally realized what was going on. He had arranged a special luncheon to announce her retirement and to thank her for her many years of work with the APRA. The number of people who attended attested to Jeanine's reputation with the organization across the country.

As in her personal life, Jeanine was a self-effacing person professionally. Initially, she felt uncomfortable with the accolades heaped upon her. Then, after the open mike session ended and the meal was finished, Jeanine agreed to say a few words.

When she reached the lectern, Alan presented her with a piece of sculpture by a young Chicago-based artist. The sculptor herself was in the audience. She came to the podium and explained how the APRA had made a significant impact in her life. The young artist almost cried when she talked about the APRA's intervention when her insurance company threatened to withdraw benefits after a particularly long hospitalization. The APRA had successfully defended the artist. Every state chapter of the APRA cited the landmark case.

Jeanine accepted the sculpture – a miniature bronze depicting the skyline of Chicago. She knew she would find a special place for it in her home. She spoke of the years she had spent working to improve the communication between patients and hospitals and physicians. Even without a script, Jeanine spoke from her heart about her work. Her initiatives had helped countless patients regain both power and dignity, even earning grudging admiration from medical professionals.

Throughout the luncheon, Lauren watched her colleague and friend closely. She knew first-hand what Jeanine had accomplished at the APRA, but she was still taken with the modesty Jeanine displayed when person after person took the microphone to relate an anecdote about her influence and accomplishments. It was long past dessert when Alan asked Lauren to wrap up.

"We're all here to thank Jeanine for her efforts on behalf of patients' rights across America. The fact that so many of you chose to attend this luncheon on such short notice is testament indeed to Jeanine. The fact that you all managed to keep it a secret is miraculous." A ripple of laughter went through the room.

"As someone who's worked very closely with Jeanine for many years, I want to add my thanks to her for advancing the cause so well. Jeanine and I have become more than just colleagues. I am also proud to call her a friend. So in both capacities, and on behalf of everyone here - and of patients everywhere - I want to wish her well. I know that Jeanine will be putting her talents and skills to work in other areas and that a whole other group of people who don't even know what is headed their way will be the recipients of this remarkable woman's considerable skills and passion." Lauren paused to look around the room; she caught Jeanine's gaze as she concluded. "So let's all wish Jeanine the best of luck as she leaves the APRA and takes on the rest of the world."

The last-minute change in schedule to accommodate the surprise event for Jeanine meant moving a luncheon with the head of Theta Labs to the only other time slot available, after the official end of the conference.

John Bell-Kingsley was Chairman of the Board of Theta Laboratories Corp. Lauren always wondered whether the abbreviation for the company was intentional. John was evasive when Lauren first asked him about the company name. Certainly, the firm used the marketing advantage it offered, particularly in direct advertising to the public. After all, who could resist some TLC?

John and Lauren first met when she still lived in Boston, not long after her move there from Chicago. At the time, John was President of a company that was a major supplier of medical devices to Massachusetts Children's – and almost every other large hospital in the country. In the years since, the company had grown exponentially. Through a series of mergers and acquisitions under John's leadership, TLC had expanded its product line to include a wide range of health care equipment, pharmaceuticals, diagnostic testing and other, related health care supplies and services. They had even started providing temporary and contract staffing. There was hardly an aspect of the health care system that TLC did not sell to or service.

John was a classic example of a Type-A personality. He lived a fast-paced life, working hard and playing hard. When he met Lauren, he was still drinking and smoking heavily, until both the times and a mild heart attack convinced him to change his lifestyle. In 1990, with a slate of more-than-competent CEO candidates available from the companies he had taken over, John selected his own replacement. He had been an ex-officio Board Member for years and when he left active day-to-day management of the corporation, the Board elected him Chair.

The relationship between Lauren and John began innocently enough, at least on Lauren's part. TLC was introducing a new asthma inhaler designed specifically for children. Lauren became involved when the company's head of marketing approached her to use Massachusetts Children's as a demonstration site. The apparatus had already passed regulatory tests with the FDA. TLC was about to roll it out with an army of drug representatives ready to descend on pediatricians and asthma specialists in hospitals and their offices.

Lauren listened to the marketing head's pitch for Massachusetts Children's to take advantage of what he called a leading-edge opportunity. She was not convinced that this inhaler was any better than its predecessors were and she was concerned about how much more costly it was. They struck a deal. TLC agreed to create a prototype of the inhaler designed specifically for left-handed children and Massachusetts Children's would distribute it through their outpatient respiratory disease clinics. Lauren was satisfied that this concession from the company was an important one. She had heard complaints and concerns that left-handed children were not receiving the appropriate dosage because it was awkward for them to grasp and push the inhaler properly.

When the marketing head reported back to the company president, John insisted on meeting the person who had driven the bargain. He flew into Boston to take Lauren out to lunch, along with TLC's head of marketing and Massachusetts Children's head of Respiratory Medicine. The four of them ate in a private dining room at the Marriott Copley Square.

After the second round of martinis, the conversation turned away from business. Lauren was finding it difficult to hold up her end of the conversation. The others, all men, did not seem to be in much of a hurry to finish the meal and Lauren's attention began to wander. She was brought back abruptly when she heard her hospital colleague mention that she had lived in Chicago for two years. John asked her about that. "I went to graduate school at the University of Chicago. I really loved that city and I miss it. I haven't been back since 1975."

With the meal finally ending, Lauren stole a glance at her watch. It was almost 2:30. John was settling the bill when he asked, "I flew in on the corporate jet. Why don't you come back to Chicago with me for dinner? I promise the pilot will fly you back to Boston at a reasonable hour."

Lauren was stunned. She had never had such an offer before. Surely it was above board, as John invited her in front of the others. "Oh, um, sure," was all she could manage to say. Her physician colleague looked at her strangely. So did the marketing head. "I mean, I'll just call the office to tell them not to expect me back today. I probably couldn't function very well after these martinis anyway."

They left the hotel and headed directly to Logan airport. Lauren had never before seen the area of the Boston airport reserved for private jets. The departure lounge was small and quiet, compared to the public gates she was used to. There was no loudspeaker system continually interrupting with announcements she could not decipher. They paused only long enough for the pilot to file the flight plan, then they were off.

John and Lauren were alone in the passenger cabin of the Lear Jet. The plane was decorated in a very masculine clubby way. The TLC monogram was woven into the fabric of the seats and etched onto the glasses in the fully equipped bar. As soon as they seated, the pilot began to taxi. They took off without delay and quickly reached cruising speed of 500 miles per hour.

They landed at Midway Airport in under two hours. They had spent their time talking about favorite spots in Chicago and learning more about each other. Lauren's story was simple. She glossed over her childhood in San Francisco and her time at Berkeley. She had been a student for most of her life and had only been in the working world for two years, so there wasn't much to tell about her career.

John turned out to be twenty-one years older than her and his history was proportionately more complex. He had spent most of his corporate life with TLC and now that he served as Board Chair, it was unlikely that he would be associated with any other company. The non-competition clause was too tight. Besides, the stock options were too good.

On a personal note, John had been married and divorced years earlier. He paid significant child support for his three children and even more significant alimony to his ex-wife. The numbers he bandied about were monthly figures about equal to Lauren's annual salary. John was only half joking when he told Lauren that the happiest day of his life was about to happen. "My ex-wife is getting remarried and I can finally stop paying alimony. I don't even know the man and I am grateful to him."

Lauren accepted that a company car was waiting for them when they deplaned. Nothing about this day could surprise her. The chauffeur took them directly to The Palmer House for dinner. Of course, they had a premier table at the Lockwood Restaurant. "Good evening, Mr. Bell-Kingsley," the maitre'd greeted them. "Your table is ready." The last thing on Lauren's mind was more food or drink. She felt as if she had been eating all day.

John saw the look on her face when she glanced at the menu. "Why don't I just order something light?" He asked the waiter to bring them Cesar salad with grilled romaine. It appeared a few moments later, accompanied by a chilled bottle of Pinot Blanc. Lauren nibbled at her salad and left her wine untouched. She looked across the table at John and asked herself what she was doing there, with a man old enough to be her father.

John watched her for a time, then rose abruptly, walked around the table and pulled out her chair for Lauren to stand. "Right. We have both had enough to eat today. Why don't we try a walk toward the Art Institute before I call the pilot to get you home to Boston?" They were out on the sidewalk before Lauren could apologize for ending the meal.

"John, I'm sorry for being so rude. I just feel I'm a little out of my league here with you."

He looked at her, then took her arm and laced it through his. "Don't worry about it. We will take this as slowly as you want. But you should know that I am not used to not getting my way. Consider yourself forewarned."

Lauren stopped walking and turned to face him. "If we're going to get along, you'll have to learn that I can be as stubborn as you apparently are. Remember, I'm the one who made your all-powerful company retool to create an inhaler for little lefties."

"Think what you will, Lauren." He liked her feistiness but knew enough not to tell her that the idea had been discussed earlier in the design stage. Her thinking was not as novel as she believed. "But if it hadn't been for those dyslexic asthmatics, I wouldn't have had the chance to invite you out to dinner."

They walked some more, again arm in arm. After a while, they returned to the hotel, where the company car was waiting. They drove back to the airport in silence. Lauren felt like Cinderella as the pilot welcomed her back into the jet for the return flight to Boston.

With the time change, it was well past midnight when Lauren turned the key in her apartment door lock. It had been quite a day – and quite an evening, too. She went directly to bed, then lay awake reviewing the events of the previous twelve hours. How had a business lunch turned into an interstate jet-setting trip of who-knows-how-many miles, just to not eat the dinner put in front of her? She fell asleep thinking how John radiated power. She had never met anyone like him before.

The next time Lauren heard from John, he called her at home. She wasn't hard to find. They had talked about where she lived and her number was listed in the telephone book. "John – what a surprise," she stammered when he identified himself. Her first reaction was to ask if he was back in Boston. "Where are you calling from?"

"I'm in Chicago, where I belong. But not for long. I'm flying down to Denver on business and I'd like you to join me for the weekend." Lauren did not know what to say. "You told me you'd never been there," John reminded her. "So what's stopping you?"

"Good question," Lauren admitted. "To start, there's the number of - "

John interrupted. "I've booked a flight for you leaving late Friday afternoon. And don't worry; I've also booked a separate room for you."

How did he know? "Um, I'm not sure," Lauren replied, amazed that he had read her mind.

"I told you I like to get my own way," John laughed. "Your airline tickets and hotel confirmation will be delivered to you at the hospital on Thursday. Don't worry, they will be in a plain brown envelope. Sorry I can't send the jet, but commercial will have to do. I will be at a late meeting, so don't expect me to join you for dinner when you arrive. I'll see you on Saturday morning."

"Don't I have a say in this?" Lauren asked.

"Not really," John replied. And he hung up.

Lauren had two days to decide whether she would go. She debated endlessly with herself, imagining leaving a message with John's office in Chicago that she had changed her mind. She would have to be very circumspect. She could not very well say, "Please tell Mr. Bell-Kingsley that Lauren Saunders from Massachusetts Children's called. I'm terribly sorry, but I can't make our appointment." His secretary would want specifics and would not be able to find any meeting with her in John's calendar. Besides, it sounded so lame.

Friday saw Lauren on the flight; it was the first-class ticket that told her John was determined. She was not at all surprised to deplane and see a driver holding a sign with her name on it. John had arranged for a car to pick her up for the drive to the hotel. And John was true to his word; the reservation clerk told her that her room was prepaid for two nights.

Lauren was tired from the long flight and went straight to her room. Another surprise greeted her. The coffee table held a bouquet of flowers and a bottle of mineral water tied with a bow. The note was from John, "I didn't want you to think I was plying you with liquor."

John and Lauren met, as planned, the following morning. "I'm so glad you decided to accept my invitation," John said, with a hint of a smile.

"Well, you made it very tempting. And thank-you. So far, it's been perfect."

"So far? The weekend has just begun. I'll try not to disappoint."

He did not. John knew Denver inside and out and he was an excellent guide. He gave her what he called the sampler tour. They spent their two days together seeing some DAM good art, as the locals call their gallery. They enjoyed ethnic food in the historic district. And they visited the Botanic Garden. People acknowledged John wherever they went; waiters knew him and the staff at the hotel practically bowed when they saw him. Lauren was mesmerized by the power he exuded. It was like an aphrodisiac.

All weekend long, John was polite and gentlemanly. He always offered his arm when they walked, but that seemed to be the end of the physical contact between them. On Saturday night, after dinner, he walked her back to her hotel room then turned to go to his. Lauren was surprised to find herself alone in her room again. She had expected a pass from John. There had been many sexual innuendos, but Lauren concluded that she had been imagining things.

John and Lauren rode out to the airport together on Sunday. When her flight was announced, Lauren thanked John for the weekend. "I'm really glad I took you up on your offer, John. I had a wonderful time." She turned around just before boarding, "And thanks for being such a gentleman," she added as an afterthought.

"This time," John said, with a smile.

Several weeks later, John called again. "Where are you calling from this time?" Lauren asked.

"Chicago again, but I'm heading to San Francisco on business in a few weeks and I wonder whether you could show me around your home town."

Lauren could not picture running into anyone she knew and having to introduce the man whose arm she held. "It's a little too close to home, methinks. But what about the Napa Valley instead? It's so beautiful at this time of year."

"Wine country sounds good; slightly fewer tourists. Have you visited the only American champagnery? Just don't tell the French..."

John told her that he would again have her tickets delivered to her office. He did not specify whether hotel reservations would be included. And she did not ask.

Lauren arranged to take the Monday morning off so that she could have a full weekend with John. She flew out of Boston on Friday afternoon and he picked her up at the airport in San Francisco. To her surprise, the driver did not head out to the highway. Instead, he dropped them off at the cruise ship terminal in the city. Lauren did not know what to think. They were met at the dock by a representative of the small ship that cruised from San Francisco to wine country. As they chatted, the casually-dressed crew transferred their luggage to their stateroom.

John and Lauren boarded and the ship set sail soon after. The crew wasted no time in serving some local wines on deck, as they passed under the Golden Gate Bridge. Lauren had never seen the skyline from this perspective. It was magical, with the lights of the city dotting the black sky.

There were 18 other passengers, a diverse group, mostly from the U.S., with two couples from Canada. They mingled and introduced themselves until the steward called everyone in for dinner.

The ship itself was outfitted mostly in mahogany. The cabins were small but beautifully appointed, each with its own head, sink and shower. John and Lauren found their cabin – there was only one – and changed for dinner. Lauren was glad to get out of her travelling clothes.

Seating was casual. The captain joined the group for dinner and gave an amusing account of the ship's history. He explained the ground rules for the next two days in few words: relax, sip, enjoy. His only serious note concerned a required safety drill after dinner. When that was over, the passengers came back inside. Coffee, desserts and dessert wines were served while a local trio played very danceable music. Lauren found herself on the floor with John. He was a good dancer who led superbly; he did not seem to notice her occasional stumbles.

Lauren slept extremely well in the small bed. She attributed it to the long flight and everything she had to drink. Even if John had other intentions, she had fallen asleep the moment her head hit the pillow and she slept soundly until he pulled back the curtains the next morning to let the sunshine into the cabin. He brought her coffee and a croissant, then left her to go back up on deck. The galley crew had placed a small bud vase on the tray, holding sprigs of freesia.

After a quick shower, Lauren joined John and the other passengers. She discovered that they were travelling up towards the mouth of the Napa River. The ship was just small enough for the waterway. When she stood on the deck, it seemed to Lauren that she could reach out and touch the banks on both sides. After lunch, the ship anchored, as it could go no farther up the narrowing waterway.

The passengers disembarked and walked a few steps to a waiting tour bus. True to John's promise, their first stop was a champagnery. The tales of the champagne turner fascinated Lauren; she had never realized all that went into the creation of bubbly. They sampled several different types of champagne, learning about the various state occasions that had featured the different varieties. John bought several bottles when they left. The champagnery would ship them directly to his home in Chicago. Lauren would learn later that he had diverted two bottles to her in Boston. He was proving to be a man with many hidden talents.

The champagne worked its magic on the passengers and many of them dozed en route to the next stop, a winery in Napa. Not John. He was full of energy. He paid attention to the tour guide and absorbed the information with ease. Lauren was more easily distracted. It was not so much the wines that she enjoyed as the physical settings and history behind the vineyards. At their first vineyard stop, she learned the rags-to-riches story of the winery's owner, now an international art collector who displayed his collection throughout the buildings and grounds. The lawn at the entrance featured an original Picasso sculpture the size of Lauren's living room and the tasting room held an enormous Calder mobile suspended from the cathedral-style ceiling. The span of the piece must have been at least twenty feet.

By the time the bus returned the passengers to the cruise ship, everyone was ready for a nap. Lauren and John went to their cabin and quickly fell into bed. John awoke after a half hour or so and went out on deck while Lauren continued to sleep. She awoke, showered again and chose a new outfit for the evening, before finding John in the lounge, chatting with other passengers.

Before dinner, a vintner from the area gave a talk on local varietals, offering samples from his own collection. His wines were featured with dinner, prepared from local ingredients purchased that day. No detail was spared for the passengers' enjoyment.

The second day on the cruise featured Sonoma. In addition to another winery, the group stopped at an estate that bottled brandy. The guide warned the group about the fumes in the aging room – actually a cavernous space about half the size of a football field, filled with row after row of oaken barrels. When Lauren walked in, the brandy vapors overpowered her. John helped Laura outside when she became faint; it took her several hours to get over the contact hang-over.

After the drive back to the ship, Lauren felt better. She joined John and the others on deck as they approached San Francisco, reversing their trip under the bridge. They docked in late afternoon and had just enough time for dinner before heading to the airport for their flights home. Lauren took the Sunday night overnight flight, arriving in Boston in time to be back at work on Monday afternoon. How effective she was at the office was anybody's guess.

When she finally returned to her apartment that evening, she was exhausted. She had had a wonderful weekend with John. She still was not sure what their relationship was all about, but was enjoying his company more and more and really was no longer aware of the age difference between them. In fact, thinking back to the cruise, she realized that John seemed much more energetic than she was. Her thoughts were reinforced when the champagne arrived a few days later, with a note that read, 'Perhaps this is the tonic you need to stay awake.'

A pattern developed between Lauren and John. He rarely called her just to chat. When he did phone, it was to invite her to meet him somewhere. They didn't spend time together in either Boston or Chicago. They took trips to Detroit and Dallas, to Phoenix and Portland. They stayed at 5-star hotels, at luxurious resorts and at historic lodges. From time to time, there were awkward moments when someone assumed that they were father and daughter. Lauren and John brushed aside these incidents; they enjoyed each other's company too much. Besides, John was young when it counted.

When they became lovers, he taught her things about sex that she had never experienced before. His lessons were not restricted to the bedroom, either. He subtly tutored her in business as well. John introduced her to Fortune 500 Presidents and to senior politicians in Washington. He was never paternalistic, nor were the people she met through John, who always treated her with respect.

John also gave her stock tips, which she followed to her benefit. After she made a small fortune investing in a company that was about to market a revolutionary product - contact lenses - she wondered fleetingly whether she was somehow guilty of insider trading. John seemed to know what was about to be the next big thing and he shared his information with her when they were together.

Their relationship grew stronger each time they saw each other. They both realized that spending time together in hotels was one continuous fantasy, but because they lived so far apart, it was difficult even to consider anything more real.

John had warned Lauren at the outset that he always got what he wanted. During a trip to Washington, DC, he told her what that was. They had been seeing each other for almost two years and John wanted Lauren to move to Chicago. It was impossible for him to leave that city and he wanted her closer. Lauren did not know what to think and John was not any more forthcoming with his definition of 'closer.'

She had been at Massachusetts Children's long enough to be ready for a new challenge, but she was not sure which direction she wanted to go. "I hadn't thought about moving back to Chicago. If I do leave Children's, I'm not sure I want another hospital position. I know it sounds bizarre, but I realize that I do not like hospitals much. I might consider going back to school. I've been thinking about studying law or even working on a Ph.D."

"Well, I'm sure the University would be happy to take you back. But you are just getting going in your career. You told me that you were tired of always being a student. Are you sure you want to do that again?" He had a way of getting to the heart of the matter very quickly.

"Besides, if you don't want to stay in hospital management, there's always organization work. And Chicago is the headquarters for so many healthcare and medical groups and associations. I am sure you could find an interesting job in one of them. I know that the American Patients' Rights Association is looking for people. I meet with the senior staff at their conference every year and Alan Forester, who is the President, was telling me about their current strategic plan. They are expanding and have some interesting initiatives in the works. Why don't you get in touch with him? Mention my name if you want to."

"Let me think about it, John." She smiled at him across the table at the restaurant in Georgetown. "Please don't pressure me too much about this. There's a lot for me to consider."

Several weeks passed before John raised the subject again. Lauren had been thinking about all the possibilities that moving to Chicago might raise. She discussed them with Louisa, who knew the most about John. Ultimately, she also told the whole story of John to Marjorie, Gwen and Andrea, when the women got together for dinner after work.

Lauren had always been leery of mentioning John to Marjorie, perhaps because they were so close in age. She need not have worried. Marjorie had met John years earlier and was a big fan of his. She was delighted that Lauren had John in her life. Gwen, too, thought the situation was a good one. "You've had two years to get to know each other. And if you could share a small cabin on that cruise ship in California and not get on each other's nerves, you must be at least somewhat compatible."

"I say, go for it." said Louisa. "You know, my father is 13 years older than my mother and they have a great marriage," she continued.

"Marriage? Who is talking about marriage? I am talking about moving to another city, about possibly going back to school, and about leaving hospital management after a very short career. Isn't that enough? When did marriage enter the picture?"

"You're dealing with John Bell-Kingsley," said Marjorie. "He gets what he wants. You know that. He would not ask you to move to save on long distance telephone charges. Come on, Lauren. You must have thought about a future with him."

Lauren was uncomfortable and tried to steer the conversation in another direction. "I did take John's advice and I called the APRA. When I mentioned his name, I got through to the President right away. He really is looking for staff and he was interested in my Massachusetts Children's experience. I'm flying out for an interview; I want to find out more about what the organization does and where I might fit in."

That fall, Lauren relocated to Chicago to work for the APRA. Initially, she moved in with John. They both recognized fairly quickly that it was a mistake. His home was in Lake Forest, a beautiful community, but a long commute for Lauren. John still lived in the house he and his wife and children had shared. There was no room for Lauren's few pieces of furniture, which ended up stored in the garage. John's children were not comfortable with Lauren and she did not know how to relate to them. Worst of all was that John continued to travel, but because Lauren was new at the APRA, she did not have the vacation time to join him on his trips. She disliked being in the house without him.

In the new year, they agreed that Lauren should find her own place. John helped her relocate to the city, where she house sat for a professor and his wife who were away on sabbatical. It brought Lauren back to Hyde Park, where she felt a sense of familiarity from her student days.

After she moved, Lauren and John saw each other less and less. And when they did, they were more like colleagues than lovers. They stopped seeing each other entirely when Lauren met Richard. Throughout her marriage, the only exception was the traditional luncheon at the APRA annual conference.

After the APRA conference that featured Jeanine's surprise luncheon, Lauren invited John out for lunch. They agreed to meet at the dining room of the downtown campus of the University of Chicago GSB. It was a beautiful setting on the Chicago River, convenient for both of them. Besides, lunch was a defined period of time and Lauren wanted to be sure she had somewhere to go after the meal.

"I wanted to tell you what's been going on in my life, John. I don't know why, but when I saw you at the APRA luncheon in San Diego, I decided I had to see you privately."

"Is something wrong?" John asked.

"No, not really. It's just that after I moved out of your house, my life took a path that you know little about. And now, before I get involved in another romantic adventure, I wanted to touch base with you again."

"Remember, I told you never to discuss your love affairs with other men," John reminded her.

"This wasn't a love affair. It was a marriage. You know that." The conversation stalled.

"John, I didn't ask you to lunch to argue with you. I asked you because I want to know how you are doing and because we have not had a personal conversation in years. Is that so wrong?"

John reached across the table and took her hand. "Of course not, Lauren. It is just that there has been lots of water under both our bridges since we were together. The timing just was not right for us then. And I don't know if you are asking, but the timing isn't right for us now, either."

"What's that supposed to mean?"

"I'm not a young man any more, Lauren. I know that I used to be able to keep up with you. No, let me rephrase that. I used to have more energy than you did. But that is not the case anymore. Maybe all that hard living has caught up with me."

"John, I'm not asking you to get involved with me again. Why are you talking as if you are on death's door?"

"It's not a health thing. Just had a check-up and I'm fine." He paused before continuing. "It's because I've been living with someone for several years now. She is a great woman, closer to my age – was married to one of my racquet ball friends for years. When he died of prostate cancer, I spent some time with her and one thing led to another. And here we are." John pulled his hand away from Lauren's.

"I'm happy for you, John. Really. It's about time you started acting your age." Lauren was quiet for a moment, as they ate their meal. "Remember the first time we ate here in Chicago? I acted like a two-year-old and you were so gracious. I've never forgotten how well you handled that situation and how poorly I did."

"Look Lauren, you told me you were out of your league and you were probably right. But it did not matter, and you were a quick study. I got such a kick out of being with you. You made me feel young, true. But you always kept me on my toes, so it wasn't as if I was having a fling with some sweet young thing with nothing between her ears."

"Better quit while you're ahead. There is something I want to tell you, though. Remember when we met in Portland? You were on your way home from a trip to Japan and you brought me those beautiful pearls - the very ones you see around my neck today." Lauren pulled back her shirt collar to reveal the necklace. "I never told you what happened with them. The short story is, you owe me ten bucks."

"And the long story? What's that going to cost me?"

"How about a second cappuccino?" The waiter disappeared with their order. "What happened was that the next time I went to Europe, I decided to take the pearls with me. When I got to the airport, it occurred to me that I might have trouble bringing them back into the U.S. without declaring them, so I asked for a customs certificate showing that I already owned them. That was my first mistake."

"Just your first? I have a feeling I won't like the next installment."

"Well, the customs folks asked me where I had bought the pearls and I said they were a gift someone brought me from Japan. Then they wanted to know if the purchaser had paid duty on them when they were brought into the country." Lauren paused and smiled. "I told them I had no idea. How the heck was I supposed to know? Customs seemed quite reluctant to give me proof of ownership, but in the end, they did. I still have the green card in the pearl case."

"What happened next?"

"Well, sometime after I returned from my trip, there was a knock on the door one Saturday morning. There were two Customs Agents standing there. They actually flashed badges at me, just like on TV. When they came in, they told me they were there about the pearls. Honestly, you would think there were better uses for our tax dollars. But they were kind of cute...

"They told me that I had to prove that duty had been paid. I told them that I no longer was in touch with the person who gave them to me. John, do you realize that I covered for you?"

"Clearly I'm in your debt. I have no recollection about paying duty. Given how tired I was after the flight from Japan, I probably even forgot the pearls were in my suitcase."

"Ignorance is no excuse in the eyes of the law," Lauren pronounced with mock seriousness. "Well, two weeks later, my two Customs buddies returned. They had given me 14 days to contact my former jewelry friend. I'm sure they conjured up all kinds of theories as to who you were and what our relationship was. When I told them I had not been able to find out about the duty question, they told me they would have to confiscate the pearls to have them evaluated for duty purposes. I could get them back if I paid the fees. What could I do? I gave them the pearls and waited to hear from them."

"You realize that you are probably on a watch list somewhere now, don't you?" said John. "You mess with Customs and who knows what's next – you might exceed the speed limit or cheat on your taxes."

"I have been scrupulous about my taxes ever since, John." She smiled, remembering that John had told her paying taxes meant she earned money and that was a good thing. "May I finish the story?"

"Please do. I promise not to interrupt again."

"Well, since you asked... Eventually, the Customs guys called me. They said they had bad news. I did not know what to think. They told me that my pearls weren't real – I know they are – and that they were something called essence of Orient. In other words, they were not much more than costume jewelry. Because they were fakes, the customs charge was something like $2.42. I went down to pick them up, paid the bill and have enjoyed them ever since. I often wonder why the guys were nice to me."

"Lauren, Lauren," John smiled again. "They were playing with you. That's all. But all this begs the question of why I owe you $10. You said you paid just over $2 for the duties."

"Interest and mental duress."

"It's a deal," John said, pulling a ten-dollar bill from his wallet. Lauren added it to the tip when she paid the bill and they left. It was the last time she saw John. He died three months later of a massive heart attack.

The morning after John died, the woman in John's life called to tell Lauren. She sat at her desk, trying to absorb the news. She kept thinking about their last conversation and wondered what it was that had encouraged her to invite him out to lunch, after so many years.

Lauren was glad they had had their final talk, even if at the time neither of them realized it would be their last. She was also relieved that she knew about John's woman friend, otherwise, it would have been even more of a shock to hear from her. But what surprised Lauren even more than the phone call was the request that came with it.

A week or so before he died, John had read an article that spurred him to arrange all the details of his funeral service, complete with a handwritten note saying that he hoped the plans wouldn't be used for a long time. He listed the people he wanted the woman to call; Lauren was one of them. To her surprise, John requested that Lauren do a reading at the funeral service. It came as a complete shock that John would ask such a personal favor, but there was no way she could refuse. She was concerned that people at the funeral would guess that she and John were more than just business colleagues. They would not know that had been long ago. But did it really matter what others thought?

The service was on Valentine's Day. Lauren thought there was a certain irony in that. The chapel was overflowing with business colleagues, friends and politicians and, of course, John's children and their families. The woman he lived with was there, as was John's ex-wife and her husband.

Lauren arrived with Alan Forester and other staff from the APRA. She had not told any of them that she was going to participate in the service. She was not sure where she should sit, but managed to stay fairly close to the aisle, even though they were farther back than she thought she should be. Lauren did not want to make a grand entrance when her part came.

It was only when the service began that Lauren felt the shock of seeing the draped coffin at the front of the chapel. When the hymns and prayers started, she thought she was going to pass out. Alan saw the look on her face and whispered, "Are you OK? Do you want some air?"

It was all Lauren could do to shake her head, no. She tried to concentrate on the minister's words. Then he called her name. She took a deep breath and rose to her feet. She felt the stares of her APRA colleagues on her back as she walked to the front of the chapel. She knew that the rest of the people there were wondering who she was. The minister stepped aside for her to stand behind the lectern. Lauren's hands trembled as she smoothed the page in front of her. She glanced up at the people assembled, nodded briefly to acknowledge John's children and partner, then began to read the article from *Psychology Today*.

The May-December Couple
People in relationships with more than a 10-year age gap face frequent public scorn... When it comes to social disapproval, people who love a much younger or older

partner face discrimination as intense as that encountered by interracial and same-sex couples.

...People in relationships with more than a 10-year age gap face frequent public scorn in the form of disapproving stares or poor restaurant service. It's one of those biases that people find justifiable...

Social disapproval can doom a budding romance because partners have fewer opportunities to 'invest' in the relationship. Just as a woman dating outside her race may feel uncomfortable bringing her boyfriend home, so-called 'May-December' couples tend to receive less support for their unions than other couples do.

Despite these hurdles... age-discrepant partners are often more committed to their relationships than partners who are closer in age... They probably evaluated the costs going into the relationship.

Women are most likely to bear the brunt of society's reproach. Younger women are seen as gold diggers, while older women are scorned for trying to hang on to youth... Either way, men get a pat on the back.

There was total silence when Lauren finished reading. She kept her eyes down when she returned to her seat. The piece was as confusing to her as it was to everyone else.

Lauren chose not to attend the grave-side service but did not return to the office with her colleagues. Alan never mentioned the reading.

Why did it take someone's death to bring up issues that they never discussed before? Lauren read and re-read the *Psychology*

Today piece, even looking up the full article to see if the parts John had omitted helped it make any more sense. There was nothing in the author's words that explained why John chose to have this particular piece read at his service. And nothing to indicate why Lauren should read it.

The only conclusion she could come up with was that he had felt much more strongly about her than he ever let on. The Who Don'ts spent an entire evening trying to figure out John's motivation. They arrived at the same thought: either John had been in love with Lauren during their relationship or he had realized after their luncheon that he still felt very strongly about her. Or both.

Caroline thought the whole situation was quite tragic. "Imagine finally admitting at the age of 75 that you were in love with someone almost 30 years earlier. I find that really sad."

"Well, what I think is sad," said Melanie, "is that he never got to act on it. I mean, the man died right after he read that article. It's creepy."

"What's creepy was reading that article in front of all the mourners. I mean, his family was there. His kids, his ex-wife. And the woman he lives with – I mean the one he lived with until he died. I can't imagine what they must have thought about that reading."

"It doesn't matter what they thought, Lauren. But tell me something," Hélène began, "did you have any idea that John felt this way?"

"Hmmm, good question. I really do not know why I felt I had to invite John out to lunch. But ever since the APRA conference in San Diego, I knew that I wanted to see him. He is always so business-like when he hosts the APRA luncheon with Alan and the rest of the team. Even though I am no longer actually a member of the executive staff, I am invited every year, sort of by default. It never occurred to me before that John might have had something to do with that.

"Maybe it was because this year was more emotional than most, with Jeanine retiring and the luncheon for her," Lauren continued. "I really wish she were here. She might have a completely different perspective on this. I miss her."

"We all do, but she's doing well in Africa and anyway, we can email her to ask her opinion, if you want," said Melanie. "Or maybe not. Given what she went through with Henry, this might not be the best topic for her, you know."

"I suppose you're right," Lauren said, sounding unconvinced. "You know, when John and I were together, we never really discussed the difference in our ages. It was more a difference in our experiences; he had lived so much more life than I had. I found him fascinating, and you know I was always attracted to the aura of power and confidence he exuded. Then, when I came here to live with him, we just assumed our delight in each other would continue. It didn't occur to either of us that my moving into the house that used to be his wife's was a big mistake. Sounds stupid, I know, but we never did talk about it. I thought it would be nice to play house, so to speak. I mean, John's friends were always so nice to me when we spent any time together."

Hélène asked, "So what changed?"

"Let me guess," said Deirdre. "Isn't that the point of the psychology article? Probably John's male friends were jealous that he had a young woman who doted on him. And the men's wives would not exactly welcome the woman who took his wife's place, at least in their eyes. I know John had been divorced long before he met you, but maybe they were afraid they might be replaced by younger women, too."

"It wasn't just that," admitted Lauren. "It was also his kids. They were not that much younger than me. I had no idea how to relate to them and John wasn't very helpful in that regard. His solution was to see them without me."

Hélène suggested they change the subject, but the others continued to ponder the rationale behind the reading. She interjected, "What I want to know is this. Lauren, if you had realized that John was in love with you, what would you have done? How would you have reacted?"

"That's what's been keeping me up nights. When we were at lunch, he told me that our timing was off again. He said that if I was interested in reviving our relationship, he could not. That he was really too old and besides, that he was living with someone. I found that a little intense, since I was not fishing to get back together with him. You know that I'm happy to be dating Thomas." Lauren looked at her friends. She had tears in her eyes. "I guess it's sad, though, that he couldn't tell me directly how he felt."

"Well, he did tell you, but in a very bizarre way. That poor minister will never be the same, I'm sure," said Melanie, trying to lighten up the discussion.

"I'll just say one more thing about John, then, please, let's talk about something else," implored Lauren. "When I was going through the really hard times with Richard, my mind would wander to John. I would fantasize that I was divorced and that the moment I called John to tell him, he came running to help me. I actually imagined that we could live happily ever after, given that we had both grown older and presumably wiser. All of which is to say that I am as guilty as he was of not being completely honest about how strongly I felt. I am not particularly proud of that, I'll tell you. I really don't want that to happen again."

A week after John's funeral, Lauren received an email from Marjorie, her former Boston colleague. 'I know we have not been in touch much lately,' she wrote, 'but I just heard about John's death. And of course, your reading at the service. You must be devastated. How can I help?'

Emma was doing graduate work at Harvard and Lauren decided to combine a visit to her daughter with one to Marjorie. Emma was studying for exams and could only spare a few hours for her mother. They used the time to share brunch at Lauren's hotel. It was a treat for Lauren to listen to her daughter talk so confidently about her studies and her life in Boston. She was so proud of Emma.

Afterwards, Lauren headed to Marjorie's. They sat in her solarium, surrounded by plants that thrived under her green thumb. Lauren wondered what her secret was. It did not take Marjorie much time to get past the pleasantries. "OK, Lauren, tell me about John. How on earth did he choose that reading for you?"

"I don't know. I really do not. When I heard from the woman he lived with that John had listed me as a reader, I was surprised. But when I saw the piece, I didn't know what to think."

"Did you consider not taking part?" Marjorie asked.

"I didn't think I could do that to the dead. I mean, how could I say no to someone's last request?" Lauren looked at Marjorie. "Why do I feel that you're about to tell me I had a choice in all this?"

"Of course you had a choice, Lauren. You didn't have to come all the way to Boston to hear that from me."

"If I had a choice, it was too difficult for me to face. I caved," Lauren mumbled more to herself than to her friend.

"Lauren, you know that my patients were much younger than you are. I treated children. And even that was years ago. Now that I am retired, I am once again enjoying just talking to people, without psychoanalyzing them. And you, my dear, know that one of the best things I can do for you is listen. Of course," she continued with a slight smile, "that doesn't mean you can babble nonsense at me."

"Well, it's nice to know that some things haven't changed. You never let me get away with anything." Lauren smiled warmly at Marjorie. "I really didn't come here to be analyzed, but I always valued your perspective and the way you treated me. And even though lots of years have passed since I left Boston, I know that whatever I say to you, you'll take seriously."

Lauren took a deep breath and continued. "The piece on May-December relationships stunned me, Marjorie. It was difficult to read it on my own, but standing at the front of the chapel was like an out-of-body experience. And afterwards, I began thinking about how I behave in my relationships and how I really never paid any attention to that before."

"What do you mean, Lauren?"

"It made me think that I always expect the man to do all the work. That if he is smart enough and strong enough and devoted enough and so on, that if he proves he loves me enough, then and only then would I consider a commitment to him. Even John, who was so much more everything than me. I expected him to do all the work in the relationship and to hand it to me on a silver platter."

Marjorie put down the knitting she had been working on as they talked. "Don't be so hard on yourself, Lauren. From what I remember, you've been taking care of yourself for so long that it's the only way you know how to live." She paused to search for the right words. "So when someone comes along who might assume some of that role, who might take on responsibility for some of your life, of course you need to be sure that he has what it takes."

"Oh... I never thought of it that way. Thanks for that. It's something else for me to think about."

"You go right ahead. None of these theories or reactions is an absolute, you know. Thinking about them is not just a good idea, it's a necessity." The doorbell interrupted and Marjorie went to answer.

She left Lauren sitting in the solarium, pondering what she'd said. Marjorie returned a few moments later. Lauren was lost in thought and looked up only when Marjorie cleared her throat to announce her return. Standing beside her were Gwen, Louisa and Andrea, grinning like Cheshire cats.

Lauren jumped up and looked at them, completely dumbstruck. Her Boston women's group was   with her again. She was speechless. "Finally," Louisa said with a laugh, "Lauren has nothing to say. I can't believe it!"

The five women had not seen each other as a group in over 25 years. They had a lot of catching up to do. Marjorie had made reservations at The Legal Seafood House, for old time's sake. They left Marjorie's home for the restaurant and found a booth they had occupied many years before. They ordered dirty martinis and Bloody Mary's and began. All of them wanted to talk at once. Their waitress kept returning to take their food orders only to be told they had yet to look at the menu. Finally, the server made a suggestion. "It's none of my business, but if you gals don't order soon, I'll start charging rent on the table. So here is what I think. Order another round of drinks. Then get some chowder and some appies. Then main course, coffee and dessert if you have room. That's five courses. Each time I bring another course, someone else can start talking." And with that, she turned to bring the next round of drinks.

The waitress' plan worked, more or less. Several hours later, the Boston five left a hefty tip, thanked the waitress for her diplomatic suggestion, and stood on the sidewalk flagging cabs and hugging anew as each woman went her separate way. Lauren saw Marjorie home before returning to the hotel. She wanted to thank her again for arranging the dinner. It was a perfect antidote to John and his reading.

Back in her room, Lauren thought about the evening as she prepared for bed. What lives they had all lived. Lauren realized that each of them had gone down a path that was completely unanticipated when they first met.

Much to everyone's surprise, Louisa had given up the party life and had entered an order of teaching sisters. She was still extroverted and vivacious, but somehow had a calm about her that made her all the more beautiful. She explained her decision to join the church quite matter-of-factly. "I was engaged but kept leaving my fiancé stranded when I found some cause or other to champion. I finally realized that the only legitimate way a young woman could get involved in some less-than-savory issues and situations was to be a religious. My fiancé was not very gracious about it but my family was very supportive. They said they had always hoped one of the kids would enter the church. They just had not thought it would be me.

"You should have seen me when I went to graduate school in my 40s as a nun. They found accommodations for me in married student housing. My classmates were all much younger than I was and they thought that was hysterically funny. It was, actually. Anyway, they took me into their study groups and always used me as a shield when one or another of them would have to go home, drunk, to a waiting husband or wife. It was all quite endearing, really. And I always said special prayers for them to pass their exams, even when they didn't really deserve to."

After Louisa's revelation, Andrea was a little hesitant to talk about herself. She need not have worried. Several of the sisters in the house Louisa shared were in long-standing gay relationships. At least with some of the more staid and conservative superiors, they all practiced the 'don't ask, don't tell' approach. Andrea grimaced at the expression, but took it as well-intentioned.

"It was really difficult to come out to my family and to my law partners. But when I did, it felt as if such a load was off my shoulders. I could finally live the life that felt right to me, as opposed to the one everyone else wanted." Andrea paused for a moment, before continuing. "My life partner came out as a teenager, which was good and bad. She helped me understand all the stages you go through when you out yourself. But in some ways, I thought I met her too soon. When she talked about her wild gay lifestyle before she met me, I felt envious. As if I had missed all the good stuff. Let's just say I caught up to her a little bit. Now we are like two old married ladies. Except that, we are married to each other. It's wonderful."

Gwen felt her life had been quite mundane in comparison to the others. She and Chris had two more children. After the third, Gwen decided not to go back to work when her maternity leave ended. She became a stay-at-home mother and everyone benefited from it. Her three children were now married and had already given her seven grandchildren, with two more on the way. The whole family lived within driving distance and spent a lot of time together. "I'm one of the few women I know who is still married to her original husband," Gwen commented. "I must be a throwback to another era. But I really do love it."

Marjorie spoke little, only saying how content she was to have time, since retirement, to indulge in her twin passions, knitting and singing. She was very talented at the former and turned out endless sweaters, scarves, hats and blankets for her children and assorted grandchildren - and anyone else who asked. As for the latter, Marjorie had joined a group of Sweet Adelines. The performances, complete with hokey costumes, gave her tremendous pleasure and gave her family a new appreciation of four-part harmony. She still kept an office at Massachusetts Children's, where she gave the occasional lecture and sometimes led grand rounds or consulted on a particularly difficult case. But more and more, she turned down requests for her professional expertise and led a more creative life.

When she heard about John Bell-Kingsley's death and funeral, she had emailed Lauren right away. As soon as Lauren asked to visit, Marjorie began tracking down the other Boston women, to plan the surprise. Given the short time to get them all together, she was delighted at her accomplishment. It had always been a pleasure to spend time with these young women. She did not have to mother them and they did not push back when she was, very occasionally, she was sure, either overbearing or critical. Now that they were all that much older, it was as if her little chickens had come home to roost. It was a privilege to listen to their stories.

Lauren marveled at these women. Their lives had been exciting and filled with various dramas. Even Gwen's had its own appeal. The irony was that the Boston women thought Lauren's life as stimulating as theirs. When she had her turn, at coffee, she managed to summarize her life by talking about Emma and Jason. She was so proud of them. She tried to avoid mention of John, but Marjorie would not have it, so that story came out. It was followed by comments on Richard and Peter. She deflected questions about her current social life, because she did not want to go into the issues with Thomas. The others seemed to think she always had a man in her life, but it certainly didn't feel that way to her.

Lauren had not seen Thomas since the holidays. They often went months without getting together, but this time seemed longer than most. She took the initiative and invited him to dinner at her place. Miraculously, Thomas said yes.

They always had a lot to catch up on when they saw each other. Lauren planned a simple meal so that she could sit at the table and share a conversation, rather than jump up and down repeatedly to head to the kitchen. She prepared an easy fish stew, served with country-style bread and a green salad. Instead of an appetizer, she put out olives stuffed with feta cheese before dinner. They went well with the martinis she prepared – gin for Thomas and vodka for her.

When they were ready to eat, Lauren brought everything to the table. Thomas opened the bottle of Malbec he had brought. He no longer asked if Lauren preferred red or white. She had told him early on that the only time she drank white wine was when it came in a bottle with a popping cork. Otherwise, white wine gave her headaches. Thomas pronounced, "The color wars are over" and always brought red. He did not seem to mind; he could drink anything.

They spoke little when first they sat down, concentrating on the food in front of them. Thomas did not eat dessert, ever, so Lauren was not surprised that he had another serving of the stew. He helped himself to seconds from the tureen she had brought to the table.

When they had finished eating, they brought the dinner things into the kitchen. Then they sat down at either end of the sofa, positioning their bodies so that they could look at each other. Lauren extended her legs onto Thomas' lap. She could make herself at home. She lived here.

They began to talk about nothing in particular. Thomas commented on a new piece of art Lauren had purchased for the spot above the fireplace. The first time he'd come to her apartment, he'd told her that she had a highly refined taste in art, even though he thought that some of the stuff she liked was not that great. Imagine! Since then, he had learned to be less judgmental. Lauren grimaced. He thought he knew a lot about art, but clearly, Thomas' taste was quite different from Lauren's. Sepia tone prints of old cars adorned the walls of his home. "Electric, every last one of them," Thomas had proudly explained when Lauren first saw them.

The conversation drifted from art to current events, to on-line dating. They always laughed at how they had met. Thomas admitted that Lauren was the first woman he had met through brainiacs.com. Lauren noticed that he did not say she was the last. Suddenly, the penny dropped.

"Are you really as busy as you say you are, or are you seeing other women?" Lauren asked, staring intently at Thomas.

Thomas started stammering. "Well, to tell you the truth, yes, I'm incredibly busy. And yes, I'm seeing other women."

Lauren pulled her feet off Thomas and tucked her legs beneath her. "Define 'seeing.' Tell me it doesn't include sleeping with them, too."

"As the man said, I cannot tell a lie." Thomas smiled sheepishly.

"So I've been sleeping with you and by default with every man those women have slept with? Are you mad?" Lauren was furious. "Not only are you carrying on simultaneous affairs, but by not telling me, you're putting my health at risk."

"Putting your health at risk? Aren't you being a little melodramatic? Come on, Lauren, surely you realized I was not always working when we could not get together for weeks and months on end. You are a smart woman. Did you really fall for the busy routine so completely?"

"I guess the answer is yes. Call me stupid, but I believed you. But what I cannot believe is that you insisted on not wearing a condom. That makes both of us really dumb."

Thomas looked at her as if he really did not understand. "But the other women know about you, or at least that someone else exists. They don't mind. Why do you?"

"Because I expect monogamy from my partners, that's why. Even if it is serial monogamy. Look, neither of us is a teenager, but I really feel you are acting like one." Lauren stood up from the sofa, "I think you should leave."

Thomas looked more confused than surprised. Oddly enough, he did not seem upset. He put down his unfinished glass of wine, walked to the door, retrieved his coat and left "The nerve!" Lauren said to the closed door. She had not called a cab for Thomas and she hoped he had a hard time flagging one down.

She made a mental note to have an AIDS test at the drop-in clinic. Just in case.

The next day, Lauren met Deirdre for brunch. She told her about the previous evening with Thomas.

"Lauren, you're not exactly a virgin queen. Don't you think you were a bit rough on Thomas?"

Lauren shook her head as if to make sure she had heard correctly. "Surely you don't think that Thomas was right not to tell me about sleeping with those other women?"

"No, of course not. It's just that you might be acting a little hastily, don't you think?" Deirdre continued. "I mean, if there's no Thomas, what are you left with?"

"I can't believe what you're saying, Deirdre. You can't really be suggesting that I continue seeing Thomas because otherwise, I am alone. Tell me I've misunderstood you."

Deirdre looked at her friend. "Lauren, we've known each other almost all our lives. We have been through a lot together, some of it good and some not so good. I was there for you when you split up with Richard and I saw how unhappy you were. I just don't want you to go through that misery again."

"The Thomas situation is hardly the same as the end of my marriage. What are you thinking?"

"I think you were hasty, is all. I am not asking you to get back together with Thomas. I'm just asking you to think about how lonely you'll be without him."

"So I should play second – no, make that third – fiddle in his little string ensemble? I cannot even believe we are having this conversation, Deirdre. What's going on?"

Deirdre looked at her. "What's going on is that I know exactly how you feel. I have been there myself. I am there myself." She paused and looked away for a moment.

"What on earth are you talking about?"

"Do you really want to know? Russell has been having affairs for most of our marriage."

"Ohmigod, Deirdre. Why did you never tell me this before?"

"It was too painful. And too embarrassing. When I first found out and confronted him, Russ gave me the option of leaving. But he told me he would not make it easy for me. He actually enjoys being married. He also enjoys bedding every woman he comes across. There have been so many that I have lost count. Now, he doesn't even hide it from me anymore. He knows I will not leave.

"Besides, I'm used to it now. Russ and I lead such separate lives. We rarely spend time with each other, and believe it or not, when we do, we can be civil, especially if we are in public. Sometimes, we almost enjoy each other's company."

"That's horrid, Deirdre. But how does that relate to my continuing to see Thomas? Not that it's even important, relative to your story. Do you really think I'm better off with someone who sleeps around than being alone?"

"I don't know what to think any more." Deirdre signaled the waiter for more coffee. She seemed rooted to her chair. "I do know that I couldn't live by myself and I guess I don't want you to be alone either."

Lauren smiled tentatively at her old friend. Her anger dissipated as she watched Deirdre absent-mindedly stir her coffee. "Deirdre, I'm sorry that I had to hear about you and Russell this way. But I am glad you shared it with me. Any time you want to talk about it, or any time you just need to get away, please call. I promise I will listen, without offering gratuitous advice. After all, you know what that's worth."

Deirdre managed a smile. "Thanks, Lauren. It feels better now that I have finally spoken it all aloud. You know, I have not told a soul in all the years that Russ has been cheating on me. I guess I've been cheating on myself by keeping it a secret, too."

"I guess you're not ready to tell the Who Don'ts yet, are you?"

"Oh, please no. I just could not. But it is time for me to host. So let me get on it."

They paid their bill and walked back to Deirdre's car. On the ride back to Lauren's apartment, they hardly spoke. Thomas was forgotten.

The Who Don'ts gathered at Deirdre's home a few weeks later. She told them in advance that the evening's theme would be left-overs, leaving the topic open to interpretation. It did not feel right to be meeting without Jeanine, but she was still in Africa. According to her emails and blog, she had no plans to come back to Chicago any time soon. Given a choice between the heat of Africa and the cold of Chicago, perhaps her decision was not so surprising.

When she arrived with the others, Lauren felt a little awkward seeing Russell. He was his usual gracious self, chatting and joking with the Who Don'ts as he took their coats and things. When the women were all seated in the family room, he came by with his own coat on. "I don't know the secret handshake, so I'll leave you ladies to your private rituals. I'm heading out for a while. Deirdre, don't wait up." He waved to the women as he left. Hélène, Caroline and Melanie smiled at him as they waved back. Lauren and Deirdre did not.

The women spent the first part of the evening catching up and giving each other the latest news on Jeanine. When Deirdre called them to the table, several women went to retrieve tote bags from the closet. They had taken the topic of left-overs seriously and had brought show-and-tell items to illustrate their stories.

As hostess, Deirdre went first. She pulled out a bag from beside her chair and withdrew a pair of blue jeans. They were a size 2. "I've had these since I was in university. Back then, they fit beautifully. Now, there isn't enough fabric in the entire pair to cover even one leg of mine." The others laughed. "I don't know why I keep them, but I guess they are a reminder of my youth. And I can't let go."

Caroline laughed. "You won't believe this, but I brought the same thing." She displayed a pair of frayed jeans pulled from her tote bag. "They are not size 2. I always thought that size was a figment of someone's imagination, but Deirdre just proved me wrong. Anyway, you will note the acid stains and strategically placed holes. These are from my rebel days. I know that you all won't believe that I ever had a defiant streak, but when Dave and I were away at college, we weren't always the goody-two-shoes that you think we are." The others smiled. Caroline was absolutely right that they could not imagine her doing anything that did not have the *Good Housekeeping Seal of Approval*.

"OK, Hélène, your turn," Deirdre urged.

"I didn't bring anything as dramatic as blue jeans. Actually, growing up in Paris, I never even owned a pair of jeans until university. I had to wear a uniform to school until then and the only other clothes I had were what we used to call party dresses. Frocks, I think you call them here."

The Who Don'ts had not heard that word in years. Now, it seemed that girls as young as seven or eight flaunted their bodies, when there wasn't yet anything to show off. "I'm shocked, quite frankly, at how girls dress these days," Hélène continued. "But fashion is a theme for another time. Maybe the next dinner when I host."

She held up her right hand. "I brought something much more timeless." On her ring finger, a magnificent array of diamonds sparkled in the light. The Who Don'ts had not seen this before. "This belonged to my grandmamman," Hélène explained. "I remember as a little girl, she would let me play with her jewelry box. This ring always fascinated me. Whenever I asked her about it, she was always vague, shrugging in that wonderful Gallic way."

"Is it real?" asked Lauren. "I mean, I've never seen anything so beautiful. Is it insured?"

"Bien sûr, yes, it's real! I had to have it appraised for the insurance. You will not believe this, but there are 109 diamonds sparkling here. I counted them. The setting is platinum and if I told you the value, you really would not believe me, so I won't bother. What I will say is that if I ever need a new car, I could trade this in and still have money left for gas." Hélène laughed. "Here's the story. My mother told it to me after grandmamman died and left the ring to me."

"I'm surprised she didn't leave it to your mother."

"So was my mother, Melanie. But when you hear the tale of this piece of jewelry, you might understand why grandmamman felt the ring should skip a generation."

"OK, ok, no more interruptions," Deirdre interrupted. "Let her tell the story."

Hélène passed the ring around the table as she began. Each of the women examined it, some trying it on. It was a beautiful art deco setting with an enormous rose cut diamond in the center, surrounded by diamonds shaped like arrows, others that were rectangular and still more that were round, but too large to be dismissed as baguettes. And there were plenty of those.

"It seems that during the Second World War, grandmamman had a liaison with an American soldier. It was quite shocking for the times and the small town she lived in. Not the romance part of it - you know the French - but the fact that the soldier was married and they were both Catholics. Anyway, it did not stop them.

"It seems it was a very passionate affair, even though it only lasted a short time. The soldier returned to the States – New Jersey, I think – and both he and grandmamman went on with their lives. Except for one thing. Before he left, he gave grandmamman this ring. She never knew its provenance or how he came by it in the middle of the war and she never asked. It didn't really matter, because she could not very well wear it in public. Can you imagine her working in the café with 109 diamonds on her finger?"

The ring had made its way around the table back to Hélène, who slipped it back onto her finger. She turned her hand to catch the light on the stones. "So, you see, this was left over from a love affair. It was before my mother was born, so I am not surprised that grandmamman hid the whole thing from her. When she knew she was dying, grandmamman told my mother the story of her lover. She asked my mother to find out if he was still alive, but she died before my mother could track him down. And then, it didn't seem important anymore."

The women paused between courses. "Wow, that's quite the tale," said Melanie, helping herself to dessert. "It's a hard act to follow, but here goes." Melanie showed the group a brown paper bag, split open to lie flat. It had handwriting all over it. "This is what's left over from my grief after my father's death. I know it is weird, but when he finally died of ALS, I felt almost relieved. He had suffered so much from that terrible disease. And we suffered along with him, in different ways.

"After the funeral, I needed some time to regroup. I did not want to have to do anything, but I also did not want to go anywhere touristy, like an all-inclusive resort. My travel agent recommended a place in the Bahamas called Cat Island. I had never heard of it before. It's near Grand Cayman. Just getting there was an adventure. I had to fly to Nassau and stay overnight. The next day, I got on another flight to reach the island. I swear the plane was held together with spit and baling wire.

"The woman who owned the hotel had said someone would pick me up at the airport. She neglected to mention that it would be in a two-seater plane. I am not like Lauren; anything less than a 747 is too small for me. I had been having panic attacks on the flight from Nassau, for heaven's sake. But what choice did I have? The man flying it, Al, I think, told me that driving was almost impossible, as the resort was at the opposite end of the island from the airport.

"Somehow, I made it there. I actually opened my eyes long enough to look down on the dense greenery that covers the island. Al told me that only the locals knew their way through, on the old plantation roads." Melanie paused for a sip of coffee. "Anyway, it seems that the place my travel agent found for me was little more than a group of guest rooms and a dining room. There was also an air strip and a marina. Except for me, everyone had arrived by private boat or plane. I was a minor celebrity in that regard.

"I spent a week there, getting into all kinds of situations that I would never have imagined. I even held those red thingies that the guys at the airport use when planes land and park. Honestly, it was one of the items on my life's to-do list. I helped land a plane coming in for a private wedding. I mean I did not land the plane, but I did signal to the pilot where to park. You should have seen me," Melanie continued, waving the imaginary flares in her hands.

"I also organized an impromptu bridal shower for the very pregnant woman who arrived on that private plane to marry on the island. The entire wedding party flew in with her. There was only one problem. She had forgotten her wedding dress back in Florida. Honestly, when the courier arrived, it was like the scene from *Castaway*, when Tom Hanks delivers the courier package after all those years."

"You mean Fed Ex really delivered?" Caroline was curious.

"Actually, it was UPS, but yes, they did. I wouldn't even want to guess at that courier bill." Melanie went on. "The shower was held on a boat that belonged to a couple who spent their lives cruising. Who knew that could be a full-time occupation? They had survived a plane crash in the Everglades and used the insurance settlement to become nomads. Wealthy nomads. Not surprisingly, they chose not to fly on their travels. I had not realized that people decorated their boats to that degree. Anyway, that's another story. There is only one other thing I want to tell you about my trip. And that's that I was witness to a major drug deal."

The Who Don'ts were not surprised. Melanie was always getting into tricky situations. The good news was she lived to tell the tales. "The islands are famous for all sorts of drug traffic. The DEA cannot respond fast enough when the drugs are moved from planes or boats onto trucks that take off into the dense jungle. A group of us was walking on the beach one day when a small plane landed, off-loaded onto an old truck and took off again in nothing flat. It could not have taken more than five minutes for the whole transfer. The DEA helicopter just was not fast enough. The agents actually started shooting from the air. We ran for cover. I do not have to tell you how terrifying that was.

"When we got back to the resort, Al, the pilot, came to talk to me. He offered me a gun, so I could protect myself. They thought the people left behind in the drug deal might try to use the airstrip to get off the island. The resort staff parked cars haphazardly on the runway to prevent that, but who knew what might happen...

"Anyway, I hadn't thought about that trip in a long time. When Deirdre mentioned the theme of leftovers, that story just came back to me. And all that remained from the trip was the paper bag. I started writing at the airport on my way home and the bag was the only paper available. I did not think anyone would believe the adventures I had. But they did distract me from my father's death and gave me reasons to experience all kinds of emotions again. So that is what I now concentrate on when I think of him. The left-over wasn't him with ALS, but all the other things he left with me."

Melanie looked at her watch. "Oops, I talked way too much. We have not even heard from Lauren yet and it is really late. Tomorrow is a school day, you know."

Hélène nodded. She was headmistress of the Chicago French School, a private school for girls, and she kept very long hours.

"I'm happy to call it a night," Lauren assured them all. "Besides, I took Deirdre literally and brought dessert that was left over from a catered luncheon at work today. And you've already eaten that, so I really have nothing more to add."

"That's that, then. We're adjourned," said Deirdre. "But don't forget your money. I have decided to donate to the local women's shelter. You know, those women have left some terrible situations and need all the support we can give them." The women quickly put down their ten-dollar bills. Deirdre added an extra bill, saying she was donating for the absent Jeanine. Lauren suspected otherwise.

Lauren scheduled a business trip to Dublin for mid-May. She planned some holiday time afterwards. She booked a distillery tour in Scotland, followed by a barge trip in Holland. From the ridiculous to the sublime, or perhaps vice versa.

She had kept a low profile since ending her relationship with Thomas. Although she missed male company, she really enjoyed her time alone. That was the conundrum. If only she could figure out how to live by herself yet still have someone significant in her life. It seemed to be the great question for many women her age. They certainly debated the subject endlessly.

Why was it that men seemed to have no trouble finding women, she wondered. Her thoughts turned to Thomas: imagine those other two women willing to share their lover. And what about Richard? He had remarried a few years back. Lauren hoped he was happy, but she had to admit that she was envious about how quickly he had found another partner.

Lauren sat surrounded by the Sunday *New York Times* and sipped her coffee. She always looked at the social column, because she found it amusing. Reading the pedigrees of the brides and bridegrooms, frequently going back several generations, was like reviewing a little slice of American cultural anthropology. These days, the brides had advanced degrees as often as the bridegrooms did, and many indicated that they would keep their maiden names. Shocking, really!

Some of the mothers had college degrees, but very few grandmothers did. Times certainly had changed since her university and graduate school days. Now, Emma and the other women at Harvard Business School were about equal in number to the men. No more ratios of 1:20 that Lauren had experienced.

Graduate school after the Viet Nam war had been a dicey time for women. Lauren and the other female students were at the beginning of the wave of women continuing on to graduate work and the professional schools. They were not satisfied with getting a Mrs. as their goal for college. But the old boys' clubs were not so keen on them. An alumnus of one graduate school interviewed Lauren and asked her what she would do when her husband was offered a job that meant moving to another city. Not if her husband, but when. Lauren was unmarried at the time. "But I don't have a husband," she had replied. The interviewer had just glared at her. Clearly, that was the wrong answer.

Lauren turned down a place at that school in favor of Chicago. The GSB had its own issues. The students were very bright and very competitive. Many of them had majored in finance, accounting and economics as undergraduates. They took entry-level courses in those subjects at the B-School to improve their grade-point averages. Lauren worked hard to keep up in those classes. The subjects were all new to her. Thankfully, her mathematics background stood her in good stead, but her male classmates were not pleased when she did better than they did on exams. Some were openly hostile, accusing her of taking the place of their buddies being shot up in 'Nam. As if the war were somehow her fault.

Lauren chose not to get into political debates about Viet Nam and the conscription lottery system. She had enough friends from San Francisco and Berkeley whose draft numbers had been called. In the days before CNN and the Internet, it was frightening each time the news reported another ambush. Everyone was on the alert for identification of the unit involved. Mercifully, only one of her old friends was killed, but it was one too many.

Lauren returned to Chicago from Europe in time to finish the work for the summer issue of the APRA journal. It was due out in July, which meant putting it to bed in late June. Work usually slowed down in the summer, giving her a bit of a breather before the Who Don'ts get-together. Hélène had broken with tradition, inviting the Who Don'ts to celebrate their 20th year at Père Marquette Lodge on the Bastille Day weekend in July. The women had never taken a trip together before.

Lauren looked forward to spending time out of the city in the summer. Even with air conditioning, Chicago was a steam bath at that time of year. It was definitely curly hair time. She could not fight it.

July rolled around quickly. The Who Don'ts had always shared evenings together. This was the first time they were extending the timeframe. The women arranged car pools to Père Marquette State Park just outside Grafton, Illinois. They left Chicago early on Friday for the drive down to the wonderful old lodge. They had booked an entire guest house, giving them space to congregate, without sitting on someone's bed.

Jeanine was back from Africa. The entire group was there.

Like the take-charge person that she was, Hélène had organized the entire get-together. She had sent out a schedule of activities and her own list of house rules. The Who Don'ts were thankful she had included lots of down time. Their first time all together was Friday evening, when they convened for dinner. Hélène had included a dress code among her instructions for the weekend. "One cannot celebrate Bastille Day wearing blue jeans," she had explained. "Besides, the topic is fashion, remember?" The women could not recall the last time they had been prohibited from wearing pants.

After dinner, they sat in the central lounge in the main building. There were not many guests that weekend, which suited them well. Hélène spoke first. "Do you realize that we've been getting together for 20 years now? I wonder how much money we have donated to our little charities over the years."

Caroline had come prepared. She pulled up a file on her Blackberry. "Don't worry, Hélène, I'll turn it off as soon as I answer your question. I know you told us to unplug and I don't want to risk a detention! Seriously, I went back to track how many times we have met over the years but I gave up when I realized I would have to go through old paper journals to do so. Isn't it amazing that we were actually able to lead our lives without electronic devices to keep us organized?"

"Don't get us going on that or we'll never keep to schedule." Jeanine laughed. She was the only one in the group who still used a paper calendar. She never went anywhere without her book. She had even taken it to Africa.

"OK, so I just estimated," Caroline continued. We started out meeting almost every month. That was the good old days, when life was slower for some reason. Now, we are lucky if we get together five times a year. So, if I take an average of 7 or 8 times a year over 20 years, I would say we have donated pretty close to $9,000 or $10,000 over the years. I think that's great."

The Who Don'ts raised their glasses. "To us!"

Lauren reminded them to look into someone's eyes when they toasted, to avoid the dreaded seven years of bad sex. She would never forget Peter's advice on that.

"Now you know why there had to be rules," said Hélène. "Otherwise, we'll keep getting off topic and never leave."

"And that would be a bad thing why?" asked Melanie. They all laughed.

The Who Don'ts sat quietly finishing their drinks and coffees. They were tired from the drive down and after a while, they headed back to the guesthouse for bed. Rather than drawing lots to see who would share rooms, they had put the snorers together. It was better for everyone's sanity.

Saturday morning, they slept in, then used the pool and gym while they took turns with spa treatments. By early afternoon, everyone had had a massage. They were all feeling mellow. They ate in the coffee shop then had some down time before heading out for some retail therapy. The gift shops in town offered little more than tourist trinkets, although Melanie did find an amethyst necklace that matched the color of her eyes. Caroline found another tacky magnet for her collection.

Dinner was another dress code event. It felt strange to wear cocktail dresses and heels in the middle of nowhere, but Hélène had insisted. The six elegantly-dressed women added sophistication to the otherwise very casually dressed crowd in the dining room.

The conversation finally turned to fashion. They talked about the style cycles they had lived through. Deirdre and Caroline insisted that even if they could not fit into them anymore, their left-over blue jeans would make a come-back sometime soon. "Is there anyone who really liked power suits?" Deirdre added. "I always felt ridiculous with those huge shoulder pads."

"They were awful, but thankfully before my time," Melanie said. The others shook their heads at her. Melanie always reminded them that there was a large difference in ages in the group.

"Well, I think that the worst trend was miniskirts. Or worse yet, hot pants. I mean, do we not all agree that the knees are the ugliest part of the human body? But even I wore those," Caroline admitted. "What else could I do?"

Lauren interjected. "My friend Louisa, the one in Boston who became a nun, had a novel approach to dealing with short skirts. Her order gave up the habit even before minis arrived on the fashion scene. But Louisa hated her knees so much that she continued to wear a habit, because it could be just-below-knee-length. I thought that a clever way to deal with a fashion crisis, don't you think?"

Hélène practically swooned when she talked about the '40s look. "If I could wear Channel suits during the day and those elegant '40s evening dresses at night, I'd be a happy woman. Don't you just love the feel of fine wool and the drape of satin?" Hélène sighed, "I have to wear suits to work every day and for them, I shop at Lord and Taylor, but only when they have a sale. And for all those events I go to in the evening, I rely on resale shops for my wardrobe. But a woman can always dream..."

Jeanine, dressed in an understated black silk sheath, adorned with over-sized silver link jewelry, contributed stories about the brightly colored fabrics that the women in Africa used for their clothing. "Initially, I couldn't understand why one day the women wore beautiful sarongs and the next, mismatched sweaters and skirts. What an idiot I was. Finally, someone explained to me that resale shops over here often donate left-over merchandise to relief agencies for distribution in Africa. Did you all know that?"

The conversation twisted and turned, touching on the near-epidemic of anorexia among fashion models, the extreme youth of the models, and the lack of reality in the high fashion world. Hélène talked again about how young girls dressed so immodestly. "The girls at the school wear uniforms, but that doesn't stop them from trying to make the uniforms their own. I've watched them stop at the edge of school property to roll up their skirts at the waist, turning them into minis. Of course, there's little I can do about it once they're off school grounds, but that doesn't mean I have to like it." She felt it demeaned the girls and the school. "C'est bizarre. The families send the girls to a French school, but for them it is only about language. I keep trying to make it also about French culture and the European way of life, but it's a real struggle."

Over dessert, the women turned the conversation to other travel plans for the summer. Deirdre planned to spend the month of August at their summer home in Wisconsin. Russell had told her he would not join her this year. "I have mixed feelings about being there alone," Deirdre told the group. "I'd be happy for some company if any of you can get away. It is fairly remote, but the house is right on the lake and it does have electricity and indoor plumbing. No Internet access, I am afraid. The cottagers' association vetoed bringing it in. Thank heavens."

Caroline and Dave were taking a cruise to Alaska. They planned to spend some time in Vancouver, Canada, before boarding the ship. They were considering driving up to Whistler as well. The exchange on the dollar made the whole trip extremely affordable.

Everyone else was staying put. Jeanine planned to use the summer to decide on her next course of action. She was not sure she wanted to return to Africa right away. But neither was she prepared to stay in Chicago without something to occupy her time.

Lauren said she might be expecting an out-of-town guest. "About a month ago, I received an email out of the blue from someone I knew when I lived in Boston. His name is Ian. He dated my lawyer friend Andrea for a while. I have told you about Andrea. Funny, I thought he might be gay; turned out she was. Anyway, Ian and my Boston boyfriend Michael knew each other and they came to visit me here once or twice when I first moved to Chicago. That was eons ago. Now Ian wants to come to Chicago again. I told him he was welcome to visit the city. He said it was me he wants to see."

A reporter from The New York Times had interviewed Lauren for a story on the international patients' rights conference held in Dublin. She had given a workshop for representatives of developing countries, encouraging them to build in an appreciation for patients' rights even as they struggled to overcome the inadequacies of their health care systems. The press coverage was flattering. What surprised her, though, was the number of contacts that came through it. They ranged from recruiters (she was not interested) to insurance brokers (she was already covered) to people who seemed to have nothing better to do than rant about their personal agendas.

Ian's email had been completely unexpected. She did not know him very well and was very surprised that he had read the article, much less tracked her down through it. With the backlog of work that she had faced on her return, she did not respond to him right away. In fact, she had debated about responding altogether.

The Gary weekend years ago had taught her to concentrate on moving forward, not on revisiting the past. Even though Ian was only a peripheral part of her history, she was unsure about him. She had phoned Andrea for advice.

"I can't believe I heard from him after all these years. Don't you find it strange that he wants to come to visit? And he insists that it's not to see the sights of Chicago, either."

"I lost touch with him when I changed law firms. He went into commercial and I am in family law, so we do not cross paths except at a rare law society event. Even then, we do not have much to say to each other. I think he never forgave me for being gay. You know, it's a macho thing. He couldn't change my mind."

"Who knows why he called," Andrea continued. "My suggestion, if you are asking for free legal advice, is to either drop it completely or to email back and forth and see where it goes. He is not such a bad catch, you know. I mean, I did date him way back when, so he comes well-recommended."

Lauren ultimately decided to respond to the initial email. She was amazed at how quickly Ian wrote back. After asking if she was married, he poured out his life story in a series of lengthy emails. Ian told her that he had been married twice but had been on his own for a long time. He was gearing down for retirement, having grown tired of the repeated battles in commercial litigation. As he put it, "All I do is make people angry and charge them a lot of money for the privilege. How much more money do I really need?"

Ian had already cut back on the amount of time he devoted to his legal practice. He vacationed at least six times a year, travelling the world on his own or with his daughters. He was very generous to them. He had taken up art, studying watercolors at a local junior college. He sent Lauren a jpeg of one of his renderings. He had drawn a picture of a friend's home, as a birthday gift. It had a somewhat cartoon quality to it, with rounded corners and a perspective that was slightly off. He had inscribed it, along with the time taken to sketch and color it, just above his signature.

The overall effect reminded Lauren of calendar art for realtors. It was not her cup of tea, but she thought it was a nice idea as a gift.

Very quickly, Ian's emails became quite demanding. He asked if he could come to Chicago before Labor Day. When she replied that the city had changed substantially since his last visit some twenty-five years earlier and that there were many things for him to see, he said the purpose of the trip was to see her, not the sights. It did not feel right to Lauren, but Ian was determined. He booked a flight without discussing the date with her, then sent her his itinerary via email, directly from the airline website. It was all very flattering, but the whole situation made Lauren nervous.

Ian arrived in Chicago early in August and Lauren agreed to meet him at his hotel for dinner on his first night in town. When they were at the table, he began drinking heavily. After his third scotch and water, he asked her to marry him. "What? No!" was Lauren's reply. The waitress overheard and came to the table.

"I just asked this woman... marry me... turned me down." Ian was slurring his words and sliding down on the banquette as he spoke. He pointed to his glass and signaled for another drink. Lauren was horrified. She looked at the server for help. The waitress rolled her eyes.

"Sir, I'm afraid you've had too much to drink. I have to cut you off now." With that, she turned away from the table, leaving Lauren wondering how she could get out of the situation without causing even more of a scene. A moment later, the maitre'd arrived with the check. A bouncer stood behind him. "I'm going to charge your bill to your hotel room, sir. And the gentleman behind me will see you to your room now. We'll call a taxi for the lady."

Before Ian could protest, the bouncer almost picked him up and pushed him out of the restaurant. The maitre'd turned to Lauren as he walked her to the hotel entrance. "Your cab will be here in a moment. Please don't worry about any of this. Don't take this the wrong way, but it happens all the time. If we could only figure out a way to have the sober guys propose, our reputation as a romantic place for dinner would skyrocket." He opened the door of the cab for Lauren. "He'll sober up as soon as he realizes how badly he behaved. The embarrassment will be worse than the hangover."

The maitre'd was correct. The next morning, Ian called and apologized profusely. He cited jet lag and excitement at seeing her again as excuses for his behavior. Lauren wondered how he had managed to do so well in professional circles with his inability to hold his liquor and his inappropriate behavior. Perhaps his outrageous ways served him well in court.

He asked to see her again, swearing off liquor if she would have dinner with him once more. Lauren was not having any of it. "No, thank-you," she said firmly. "I'll leave you to get a good night's sleep this evening and to enjoy the rest of your visit."

She returned to her coffee and her Sunday *New York Times* and smiled to herself. It was odd that the whole Ian situation started with the *NYT* and now it was ending that way, too. Half an hour later, she went into the kitchen to refill her cup before turning to the *Book Review*. Just then, the buzzer for the front door rang.

Lauren was not expecting anyone. She ignored the ringing, assuming a visitor had punched in the wrong apartment code on the enter system. The buzzer rang again. This time, Lauren turned on the small television in the kitchen and turned to channel 39. It allowed her to see who was at the front door. It was Ian. He was standing with a bouquet of flowers in his arms.

"Lauren, I know you're home. Please let me in." His voice was garbled by the enter phone system. Lauren could see other people coming and going through the lobby. When Ian buzzed the third time, she spoke, "Ian, I'm sorry, but you can't come in. Please don't buzz again because I won't answer." She heard him start to answer back before the system cut out. Then she saw him push through the door just as someone left the building. He was in the lobby, heading for the elevator. He did not realize that he would be unable to access her floor without a security fob.

Still, Lauren began to worry. She picked up the phone and called the concierge desk. The staff on duty had noticed Ian come in and saw him pushing buttons in an open elevator, to no avail. After asking Lauren if she wanted this man buzzed up to her apartment and hearing her very definite negative response, the concierge approached Ian. "I'm sorry, sir, but you'll have to leave. Ms. Saunders does not want me to let you up."

Ian turned on him, trying to get the elevator doors to close between them. The concierge used his security fob to override the system. "Sir, I'm asking you to leave the building. Would you like me to escort you out, or will I have to call the police?"

"Police?" shouted Ian, "Why would you call the police? I haven't done anything."

The concierge answered as calmly as he could. Other residents were gathering in the elevator lobby and he did not want any further trouble. "Then you won't mind if I call," he said, reaching for the emergency phone in the elevator cab.

Ian transferred the flowers to his left hand and swatted the phone with a powerful backhand from his right. The concierge quickly stepped aside as the phone flew out of the box and crashed to the floor of the elevator, dangling by the cord. When Ian saw what he had done, he stormed out. He pushed through the crowd that had gathered and walked quickly toward the front entrance. Half way across the lobby, he hurled the bouquet onto the floor in front of him. In his rage, he stomped over the blooms as he charged from the building.

Lauren watched the lobby scene on the intercom video system. When Ian finally left the building, she sat down, shaken. The phone rang again, startling her. She was afraid it would be Ian, but it was the concierge, checking to see that she was ok. He asked her what to do with the remaining flowers. "Toss them," said Lauren. "Just throw them away. And thanks for your help. I don't know what I would have done if he had managed to get up to my apartment."

After calming down, Lauren emailed Andrea. She related the story of Ian, the proposal, and the flowers, glad to get it off her chest. Andrea phoned a few moments later. "I can't believe that man. That's awful," she said. "I mean, I know you thought the whole situation was a little intense, but this is ridiculous. What did he think he was doing?"

"Don't ask me," sighed Lauren. "The whole thing was a fiasco from start to finish. Frightening, really. On the other hand, I do have to be grateful that I learned how crazy he is at the outset. Can you imagine if I hadn't found out until later?"

"Trust you to find something good in this mess. Next time you get one of those memory lane emails, just delete it, would you?"

Ian sent an apologetic email a few days later. He admitted that he had acted boorishly, but said he hoped that would not affect their friendship. Lauren was stunned that he thought she would agree. She was convinced Ian was even more unstable than she initially thought. Somewhat late, Lauren took Andrea's advice and then some. She deleted the email. Then she blocked future ones from Ian. Should he write again, his emails would go directly into trash and would generate an automatic response stating that his email was being returned, unread.

The incident with Ian upset Lauren more than she initially realized. For days after the flower episode, she worried that Ian had not really left Chicago and that he might be lurking around near her condominium building. With email and cell phones, you never really knew where anyone was.

She knew he could not get up to her apartment without a security fob, but still she checked through the peephole each time she opened the door to retrieve her newspaper or to leave. And she made certain to turn on the monitored alarm when she did go out, even if it was only down to the lobby to collect her mail. When she was in the condominium, she turned on the at-home security monitor. If Ian somehow found his way into the unit without an invitation, the alarm would go off. Lauren even found herself fantasizing that he would break in and have a heart attack when the siren started wailing. Then she would be truly rid of him.

Lauren knew one thing with absolute certainty. If she ever saw him anywhere near her again, she would call the police first and ask questions later. His erratic behavior made her extremely nervous. The fact that he had lost complete control was in some ways more frightening than his bizarre behavior itself. Lauren knew she could never trust him.

There was something very odd about how quickly Ian had glommed onto her. It was as if he envisioned a role for her in his life and was determined that she would act it out. He did not consider whether she wanted the part or not. He wanted to retire. He wanted to leave Boston. He wanted another wife. What about her? How could she live with someone who frightened her?

Lauren had dark dreams and even nightmares for days. In one, she saw Ian wandering through her condominium, looking frail and forlorn. He was almost ghost-like, appearing in one room and disappearing into another so that Lauren was not sure whether he was really there. Each time she came face-to-face with him, she would tell him that he had to leave. That he could not stay, that it was her home, not his. She would turn away from him, hoping he would vanish permanently. Each time, he followed her and whispered, "Lauren, there's something I have to tell you. I was HIV positive when we were together. You can't turn me out now."

Even in her dreams, Lauren knew that the words were hollow. They had never been together in any way that could transmit anything, let alone the HIV virus. The sum total of their physical contact was an awkward hug when they first met at his hotel for their ill-fated dinner. Besides, Lauren knew, even in her sleep, that she was HIV negative. She was tested routinely each time she donated blood. She had even had that extra test after Thomas told her about his other lovers. Still, the dream left her very unsettled. She did not feel rested when she got out of bed the next morning.

When she checked her inbox a few days after Ian's apologetic email, she found another email he had sent using his legal assistant's computer and email address. In it, he pleaded with Lauren to remove the bounce from his email address so that they could communicate again. He told her he wanted to come back to Chicago to make amends and to propose to her properly.

Lauren was absolutely stunned. She wracked her brain for any indication of encouragement that she might have given him, to no avail. Of course, she realized that her approach was logical and logic did not apply to a person who was off-balanced. Clearly, Ian was. Lauren added the new address to her email bounce list. She also signed up for caller ID on her land line and added Ian's phone numbers to her cell phone, so that she would know if it was Ian when the phone rang.

Sometimes, she thought the precautions she was taking were a sign of paranoia. Then flowers would arrive from Ian. He sent several dozen roses in the two weeks after his visit, with deliveries to her condominium and her APRA office. After the sixth bouquet arrived, Lauren advised both the concierge at home and the receptionist at the APRA to refuse any further flower deliveries.

At their next dinner, Lauren related the story of Ian's visit and subsequent harassment. The Who Don'ts tried to calm her down, saying Ian's persistence would pass. But Lauren knew better. She was convinced that in his eyes, Ian thought he had done nothing wrong and that she was only playing hard to get. If she would only come to her senses and take him into her life (it was hard to say 'back in' as he had not really been there before), everything would be wonderful. From time to time, Lauren considered capitulating, just to make her life easier.

John Bell-Kingsley would have counseled her that it all boiled down to price. "Everyone has one. It's just that mine is higher than most people's," he had told her in one of their discussions about corporate life. Lauren liked the second part. She wondered if she would ever be confident enough to use those lines herself. As brief as the interlude with Ian had been, it taught Lauren a huge lesson. She realized that there was no way Ian could pay her price, because Lauren would not be with him for any amount of money.

All through August, the emails from Ian continued, each time from a different address. Most times, they held increasingly dire entreaties begging her to re-open lines of communication between them. Occasionally, they contained angry rants accusing her of the vilest behavior. Yet they were always signed, 'Love, Ian.' Finally, Lauren called the police.

Lodging a complaint was difficult, for many reasons. For one thing, the threats and badgering were via the Internet and so were not considered real. There was also the fact that Ian lived in another state. After listening to her story and reading the emails that Lauren retrieved from her trash folder, the officers left. Their investigation ended with a slap on the wrist to Ian. They sent him a letter stating that as an attorney, he should be aware of applicable statutes dealing with harassment. The threat was empty, because in truth there was little the police could do. Ian clearly knew that.

The stress of the situation kept Lauren up at night. Finally, she decided to get away. She contacted Deirdre, hoping to arrange a visit to her summer home in Wisconsin. Deirdre was glad for the company.

To avoid the traffic, Lauren drove secondary highways and back roads on the Friday of Labor Day weekend. She and Deirdre enjoyed an early dinner. Afterwards, Lauren went to her room and quickly fell asleep, cocooned by the eiderdown on the guest bed. When the temperature fell after sunset, the quilt was very welcome. It was her first good night of sleep in weeks.

Saturday, the two women had a late start, making a full country breakfast that carried them through the day. The house had a huge kitchen and the two women shared the cooking, making rashers of crisp bacon, a small mountain of fluffy scrambled eggs and stacks of golden pancakes. They drowned the flapjacks in butter and real maple syrup. Their only hope was that the black coffee and fresh-squeezed grapefruit juice would somehow cut the carbohydrate overload. Unlikely, but one could always hope.

Each time one of them started talking about either Russell or Ian, the other one rapped her knuckles on the furniture closest at hand. That was the signal to change the subject. They decided when Lauren arrived that the weekend would be about them, not about the men who were causing them grief. They agreed to put down the stress of Deirdre's philandering husband and Lauren's virtual stalker. "You know, at the end of the weekend, Russell will still be cheating on you and Ian will still be sending me his insane emails. We can decide then whether we want to pick up that stress again," Lauren announced.

"Amen," said Deirdre.

Saturday night, Lauren treated Deirdre to dinner out. They drove to a local diner and had the blue plate special, meat loaf with a mashed potato topping. Fresh corn was the side dish. And, carbohydrates be damned for the second time that day, they had the best jumble berry pie for dessert. It was a house special and people came from miles around to enjoy it.

"I think I'll never eat again," moaned Deirdre when they returned to the house. "I am so stuffed."

"Don't you know that it doesn't count when it's a holiday weekend?" Lauren was feeling equally full. "Let's sleep it off and go for a long walk or hike tomorrow to put some of those carbs to good use."

On Sunday, after only juice and coffee, they set off. Deirdre led the way along a path that circled the lake. It was a beautiful walk with the trees towering above them. Around 11 o'clock, they were almost at the half-way point. The shore was no more than a few feet away and the water lapped up invitingly. "Why don't we cool off before heading back?"

"Perhaps because we're not wearing bathing suits?"

"Don't be such a prude, Lauren. This is a private lake and it's unofficially clothing optional. I am going in. Are you coming?"

They left their sandals, shorts and tees near a rock and waded in. Before they were fully immersed, Lauren looked around to check that no-one could see them. Then she stripped completely and tossed her panties and bra onto the shore. Deirdre did the same.

"I haven't gone skinny-dipping in years," Lauren shouted, splashing at her friend. "I'd forgotten how wonderful it feels."

"Didn't you tell me that you went nude bathing in Greece, years ago?"

"Lord, you have a good memory, Deirdre. I'll have to remember that when I tell you my secrets."

"You have no secrets from me, my friend. Or have you forgotten that we became blood sisters when we were about, what, five or six?"

"Something like that. And I remember how terrified I was to stick that needle in my finger. I wonder if kids still do that, with all the scare tactics about AIDS and such."

"Mind if I join you?" came a shout from the shore.

Lauren and Deirdre stared at each other, wide-eyed, then at the source of the voice. They started laughing so hard that Deirdre swallowed water and began coughing and spluttering.

The man on the shore was completely nude. His question was rhetorical. Dan was a neighbor of Deirdre's on the lake. He clearly had few inhibitions. And quite a few nice physical attributes, Lauren could not help noticing.

Dan joined them in the water. He first tapped Deirdre on the back to help her stop coughing, and then introduced himself to Lauren. "Water's great, isn't it?"

Lauren was trying to stop giggling. How would she get out of the water without exposing every part of her body? The three of them paddled around, treading water as they talked. Dan began swimming out to the float dock, motioning for them to follow. Lauren looked at Deirdre for help. Should they make a dash for the shore or join him? Either way, Dan would be able to see them in the flesh.

Deirdre could not stop coughing. "You go, Lauren. I have to get out of the water before I drown." She turned towards Dan and shouted, "Look out for Lauren. She might need some help getting up onto the dock." She winked at Lauren, and then headed for the shore.

To her surprise, Lauren enjoyed sunbathing on the dock. Afterward, Lauren and Dan walked the other side of the lake back to Deirdre's, stopping for a coffee at Dan's house. When they returned to Deirdre's, Dan was the first to spot a note on the door: 'Lauren, Gone to town for provisions. Invite Dan for dinner. He's a sweetie.'

He returned for dinner, bearing wine. When he left after the meal, Deirdre started, "Well, what did you think? Isn't he nice? Will you see him again?"

"Whoa! I just met the man. In answer to your questions, I thought it was different to meet him in the flesh, so to speak. And he seems nice. And yes, I will see him again. He invited me to the symphony next weekend, when we're both back in the city. Oh, I don't know, Deirdre, should I really be doing this?"

"The answer to that question is a definite yes." Dan is a wonderful man with nothing to hide, no pun intended. Seriously, I had mentioned to him that you were coming to spend some time with me. Of course, I praised you to the skies, but he's smart enough to draw his own conclusions."

"Don't even tell me you're playing matchmaker. My track record with men is not great of late and I do not want to put a hex on him. But he really does seem like a very nice man. Let's leave it at that."

After the symphony, Lauren and Dan went out for dessert and coffee. Dan drank very little alcohol, limiting himself to the occasional glass of wine. His moderation rubbed off on her. The good news to Lauren was that she would always be sober when with him. The bad news was that sometimes a few drinks helped her let down her guard, just a bit. The good news trumped the bad, she realized. She wanted her eyes wide open in this relationship. Thomas and Ian had frightened her too much to be trusting too soon and she did not need alcohol to cloud her judgment.

The second time Dan asked to see her, he invited her to his home for dinner. He told her that he was holding a small dinner party and would be glad if she would join them. Lauren was delighted. She said she would get there on her own, as she knew how hectic it was just before guests arrived. She need not have been concerned. Dan had everything organized.

He lived on a floating home in a small enclave near Navy Pier. The Dutch door was open at the top when she arrived. Classical music was playing inside. Lauren knocked, and hearing no response, she let herself in. "Anybody home?"

Dan appeared, smiling broadly when he saw her. "Hello Lauren. Welcome to my little abode. Please, look around while I finish up in the kitchen. I'll be right back."

What she could see on the lower level was one large room, two stories high. Dan had decorated in varying shades of blue, with different textures adding to the décor. Lauren noticed a large wall unit to her left and headed towards it. As she was looking at the photos on display, she heard a knock at the door. She turned to introduce herself and was very surprised to see Deirdre and Russell coming towards her.

Dan emerged from the kitchen as the others stood looking at each other. "Why don't I show Lauren the view from the deck? You two can help yourselves to some wine while we are out there. Lauren, here is some red for you. Bring it along. Now come and see the view."

Lauren followed Dan through the sliding doors onto the small deck. She was glad for the chance to get over the surprise of seeing Deirdre and Russell. The water was calm and the rocking of the boat was barely discernible. Dan's home was at the very end of the pier. Beyond the house, there seemed to be nothing but blackness as the river met the lake. In the other direction, the lights of the city were spectacular. It was a completely different perspective from the view she had at her condominium.

"I hope you aren't disappointed that Russell and Deirdre are joining us. I really did owe you and her dinner. And I couldn't very well not invite Russ." Lauren chose not to respond. She suspected that Dan knew nothing about Russ's affairs and she did not want to be the one to tell him. "He and I go way back. We worked at Ford together as management trainees when we first got out of grad school."

They went back inside and Dan left Lauren with Deirdre and Russ. Their conversation was stilted. "Dinner is served," Dan announced, when he returned from the kitchen. Lauren jumped up to help him, but he insisted that she sit with the others while he shuttled back and forth between the small galley kitchen and the dining area beside the wall unit.

Dan had created an Italian meal for the evening. They started with a spicy white bean soup, accompanied by hearty peasant bread. The next course featured pasta gorgonzola. "Heart attack on a plate," announced Dan when Lauren asked what was in it. "A big chunk of butter, an equal chunk of gorgonzola and as much garlic as I can find. In deference my health, I only prepare this about once a year. Glad to have you all join me for it. Bon appétit, or however that's said in Italian."

Russ raised his glass. "A bit late, but a toast to our host. He is a great friend, a great golfer, and a great cook. Lauren, don't mess this one up."

The comment embarrassed Lauren, but she said nothing. She did not want to get into a discussion with Russ on any topic even remotely related to relationships. She didn't trust herself to keep Deirdre's secret.

After coffee and dessert of tiramisu, which Dan admitted was store bought, Deirdre and Russ left. "Hate to eat and run, old buddy, but I think you two need some time alone."

"Honestly, Russ, I'm sure they don't need advice from you." Deirdre had been quiet for most of the evening and Lauren sensed that it had been difficult for her to be with her husband, pretending nothing was wrong.

"I think I can figure things out from here," Dan offered, rising to see them to the door. "Thanks for coming."

He turned to Lauren, who had started clearing the table. "Leave that for now. It won't go anywhere." He pointed to a very modern leather lounge chair and waved her over to it. Lauren fell onto it, then tipped it forward to be able to talk to Dan.

"Before you say anything, Lauren, I want you to know that I know all about Russ and his philandering. Deirdre confided in me when she came to the lake this summer. She told me I was only the second person she had confessed to, after you.

"As I told you, I've known Russ for years. He sure fooled me. I do not know what to make of this. I don't know if I should talk to him or stay out of it completely. I guess I had to invite them to see for myself. I hoped that somehow Deirdre was wrong. But I know she was not.

"I could see the way Russ looked at you that there was something amiss. He did not pay any attention to Deirdre and his comments were completely out of line. I'm sorry."

"Please don't apologize for his behavior. But it's not something I feel comfortable talking about, Dan. When Deirdre first told me, I asked her about marriage counseling. Apparently, Russ refuses. She chooses to stay with him for her own reasons. I could not, if I was in her shoes, but I am not her. Can we leave it at that?"

"Sure thing. Come on, I'll show you the rest of the place." Dan led her up the stairs to a catwalk that hugged one side of the upper level, leading to two bedrooms. At the far end, he showed her the master suite, pointing things out from the doorway. Back at the top of the stairs, there was a guest room. Lauren stepped into the room and gasped. Dan laughed and caught her as she stumbled backwards.

"That's Inga, my inflatable girlfriend. Russ and the others gave her to me for my birthday. Why they thought I wanted a life-size blow-up doll, I do not know. But they thought it was a hoot. I did not have the heart to throw her out, so I just tossed her on the bed and left her there. Almost forgot about her, Lauren."

"I should tell you about regifting," Lauren said. "I love that word. When I downsized from my house in Hyde Park to my condominium, I got rid of tons of stuff. Now, I have a new policy. The only things that can come into my apartment and stay are ones that are invited..."

Dan turned her towards him, kissing her for the first time. "I hope I'm on the guest list." He drew back before Lauren could respond. "Let's go back downstairs and relax before I get you home."

"What about the kitchen?" asked Lauren. She thought it might be a good idea to keep them on their feet.

"You sit. You looked very comfortable on the chaise longue. I can clear things up in nothing flat." He steered her back down stairs, with just the slightest pressure on her back. Lauren opted not to argue.

True to his word, Dan was back in the living room very quickly. "Lauren, I know this is quick, but would you consider spending the night? I will be mortally offended if you say no, but I would understand."

"Good. Because I have to take this very, very slowly. Can I take a rain check?"

"Absolutely. And I do understand, even if I am disappointed. Just realize that the rain check has an expiration date. Of course, only I know what that is, and we can always negotiate extensions, but I'm not known for my patience."

He reminded her of John Bell-Kingsley when he said that. Lauren did not want to make the same mistake twice. With Dan, she vowed that she would be completely honest. She promised herself not to play any games in this relationship.

Melanie chose 'what I did on my summer vacation' as the theme for the next dinner of the Who Don'ts. Lauren and Deirdre jointly related the skinny dipping story, leaving the others laughing.

"So what did the two of you talk about on the raft?" Caroline wanted to know. "And were you lying face up or face down?"

"Very funny. Actually, it seemed the most natural thing in the world to be there without a suit. There was nothing left to hide after Dan's full frontal entrance, so after a while, I did what the Victorians used to advise."

"Lie back and think of England?" asked Hélène.

"Cute, but I was thinking more of 'Relax and enjoy it.' Which is exactly what I did."

"Don't forget to tell them that you've been seeing Dan ever since," reminded Deirdre.

"It's only been twice, including a dinner that Deirdre and Russ came to. So don't get too excited. I promise a full report next time. What about the rest of you?"

"You know I spent the summer by myself at the lake. Well, not by myself, because Lauren came to visit. But without Russ is what I mean. In all the years we've been married, this was the first that he didn't spend time there with me." She paused to sip her wine. "I guess it's time to tell you why."

The other women looked at her. Lauren avoided Deirdre's eyes at first, then gave her friend a quick nod to bolster her confidence. "I have to tell you all what's been going on. I feel awful that I have not confided in you before, but I could not deal with it myself, let alone share it with you. This summer at the lake, I had a lot of time to think about my life and where it is going. And I made some big decisions."

Deirdre took a deep breath and sat up straight. "Russ has been cheating on me since the beginning of our marriage. Maybe even before."

The other women did not know what to say. It was not the kind of news that they wanted to hear.

"I found out about the first affair not long after it started. When I confronted Russ, he said that if I did not like it, I could leave. But that he would make it difficult for me. I decided to stay because at first, I guess I hoped it would stop. Then, after the umpteenth woman, Russ began flaunting his lovers. He did not even try to cover up or hide them. By that time, I did not know where to go. So I stayed.

"Lauren, you don't know this, but that evening with you and Dan was the last straw. I saw how Russ kept ogling you. Not that he would follow through, but because he knew I would not say anything. We had a huge row when we got home that night. I ended up sleeping in the guest room, then I heard him go out again around midnight. That did it.

"Even after being confronted, he went to someone else's bed. It made me feel dirty just thinking about it. I packed up some of his things and put an overnight bag in the middle of the garage floor, where he was sure to see it. When he returned, he could not get into the house itself because I dead-bolted all the doors. He pounded and pounded, but finally left. I do not know where he went and I really do not care.

"The next thing that happened was that I received an email from his lawyer the following morning. Russ wants a divorce. And true to his word, he's not going to make it easy."

"Oh, Deirdre," Melanie ran around the table to hug her. "How are you coping? Do you have a lawyer yet? I hope you find an absolute barracuda."

Deirdre wiped the tears that flowed down her cheeks. "You know, deciding to get out of the marriage was hard enough. But the legal stuff is even worse. And it's just beginning.

"Russ has always been litigious - you all know that. He has more lawyers in his contacts list than I have friends. Even finding someone to take my case is a challenge. All Russ's lawyers work for big firms and that precludes their family law people from taking me on as a client. I'm sure Russ is gloating over that."

"Don't worry about it," Lauren offered. "I'll ask my friend Andrea to recommend someone. She does family law in Boston and has a network of colleagues all over the country. I'll email her in the morning and help you find someone."

Deirdre stared down at the placemat directly in front of her. She could not look directly at the Who Don'ts. "I don't want to talk about it anymore. It was hard enough telling you all about Russ and what a jerk he has been. And I feel like such an idiot for putting up with his philandering for so many years." She sighed deeply. "Isn't there anyone who had a positive experience over the summer? Other than Lauren, I mean."

Melanie left the table for coffee, tea and dessert. She spoke when she returned. "My turn. You know, I picked the summer theme for a reason. September has always been the start of the year for me."

"Me, too," nodded Hélène.

"Towards the end of August, I always start gearing up for school. This summer, I decided that I just did not want to do that anymore. I told the school that I would not teach the adult art course for the fall semester. I just could not face it again. You won't believe what I did."

"I'll bite," said Jeanine. "It can't be anything more drastic than my leaving the APRA and going to Africa."

"I'm not sure that drastic is the right word. But what I did was something quite off the wall. My mother is apoplectic and my father is probably rolling over in his grave. I wanted a job that would be less stressful. One that did not involve lesson plans and reviewing artwork and soothing the bruised egos of completely untalented aspiring artists. Oh, and did I forget responding to the deluge of emails from the students? No more."

"Come on, Melanie, don't keep us in the dark like this. What exactly did you decide to do? I told my secret, so you have to, too." Deirdre managed to smile.

"I took a job as a door man - oops, door person - at a little boutique hotel in The Loop. The Deco. Does anyone know it?" They were too stunned to answer.

"Don't look so shocked. It is actually a fascinating job. All I have to do is wear a funky uniform, smile and open doors. I have a whistle to hail cabs and to call bellmen. And you would not believe the tips I get. And the best part? At the end of my shift, I go home. I cannot possibly take work with me. I don't know why I didn't think of this years ago."

"I don't know what to say," uttered Caroline. "I guess as long as you enjoy it, why not? And who knows, you could open the door to the man of your dreams."

"Will you never cease being a romantic?" asked Jeanine. "Maybe Melanie is like me? Not interested in finding a man."

"Speak for yourself, Jeanine. I just have not met Mr. Right yet. I'm just slower than you all are."

Hélène looked at her watch. "Ladies, Melanie has opted to leave the education calendar behind her, but I haven't. I will be brief. I can tell you that once again, I spent a few weeks of the summer in France, which is the worst possible time to go. You know, everyone goes on vacation at the same time and the roads are jammed and, to tell you the truth, it is wonderful. It makes me feel French again. Every year, I say I will not go back and every year I do. You have heard it all from me before, so I will not repeat myself. And I am sorry, but I really must leave. For me, anyway, tomorrow really is a school day." She put a ten-dollar bill on the table and left. "Don't let me end the party, but I have to go. Au revoir."

"Well, as a lady of leisure, I'm happy to continue, if the rest of you are," Jeanine announced.

"Of course, Jeanine. Go on. Have you decided what you're going to do next?" Melanie asked.

"Yes and no. I want to go back to Africa at some point, but not yet. In the meantime, there are so many needs right here in Chicago. I do not have to go half way around the world to make a difference. So what I did on my summer vacation was find something to occupy my time in the city.

"You know how much I adore my grandchildren. But they are so far away that I rarely see them. So... I have volunteered at Northside Hospital to be a baby cuddler. It is the next best thing to being a grandma because all my work entails is holding the babies. I cannot feed them, although occasionally, I do manage to burp them after their bottles. And if their diapers are dirty, I just call for the nurse. Heaven.

"Seriously, it's a special unit for babes born to addicted moms. The little things need all the hugging and touching that they can get. What a horrid way to come into the world, already fighting an addiction.

"I have two shifts a week. Each time I go, the nurses put another baby into my arms and I sit and rock the child for hours. If I had high blood pressure, which I do not, it would plummet. Really, it is such a privilege to be able to cuddle these little ones. So many of them end up in foster care, because their mothers cannot take care of them.

"At first, I must admit I had some real issues with the moms. I do get to meet some of them. And then, one day I met one of the more successful mothers. She had kept her child and was visiting the unit to show off her toddler. She came into the nursery and I suspect that I visibly pulled away from her. I have never seen anyone up close with that many tattoos and piercings.

"She sat beside me and we both rocked for a while. She started talking and told me how the unit had been such a safe haven for her. It got her off the streets and out of the sex trade. After a few moments, her son tired of exploring the nursery and crawled into her lap. She bounced him on her knee, then began nuzzling him on his tummy until he giggled. I realized then that she was like any other mother who loved her child. And I stopped seeing the body stuff and saw a young woman really struggling to turn her life around. I learned so much from her."

"Cuddling? Do they need other volunteers?" asked Caroline. "I never thought I would want to do that, because of what happened with Zara. But I think if I were to go with you, it might be ok. Would that work for you?"

"I'd be delighted. I will find out if you can join me. My shifts are late afternoon, so it should not be a problem for you to get there after work. Besides, it would be nice to have company. The nurses are run off their feet and rarely have time to chat. And since I seem to have the ability to settle just about any baby, they fall asleep on me quickly. I'd enjoy having someone to talk to."

"Aren't you going to tell us about the cruise?" asked Melanie.

"No. It's not as important as babies." Caroline looked at the Who Don'ts sheepishly. "I mean, it was fine and Dave and I had a great time. But when you get right down to it, it was lots of water, too much food, and the occasional whale, and after a while, it was even hard to remember what day it was. We had a wonderful visit in Vancouver, though. It is an incredibly beautiful city and I would definitely go back there. But another cruise? I don't think so."

Melanie called the evening to a close. "Do you remember having to write those compositions 'how I spent my summer vacation' each September when we went back to school? It's a good thing we do not have to put our stories in writing. What a book that would make."

The Who Don'ts added their ten-dollar bills to the one Hélène had left. "You probably don't know this," Melanie said as she gathered the money. "There is an international association of doormen and it raises huge amounts for charities in each city that has a chapter. I am going to donate our money to them. I'll let you know where the funds end up."

Lauren's birthday came around again far too quickly. It seemed like only yesterday that she had been with Thomas, having dinner at his home to celebrate. She grimaced at the memory of spending the night with him afterwards. And learning months later that he somewhat conveniently hadn't told her about his other lovers.

Little did she know that the Thomas episode would signal the beginning of an 'annus horribilis,' to quote Queen Elizabeth II in one of her recent New Year's greetings. To be more accurate, the year was a disaster on the man front. Thomas wanting her to play third fiddle was just the start. Then there was John Bell-Kingsley's death and the whole funeral reading episode. As if that was not enough, there was the Ian saga.

Lauren fleetingly considered swearing off men forever. Of course, that thought did not stop her from seeing Dan a few times since returning to Chicago. Deirdre was right; he was a sweetie. Maybe this year would be different.

Dan arranged a very special birthday celebration for Lauren. Through Deirdre, he had discovered not just the date itself, but some of the things that Lauren might especially enjoy.

When he arrived to pick her up, he presented her with two long-stemmed white roses. She was unsure what the color signified, but happy that they were not red. Peter had claimed that color. Thankfully, he had not sent flowers this year. Apparently, her last note to him had done the trick.

"Two?"

"Yes, one for you and one for me. Except that, you get to keep them both. I'll expect progress reports on their health and well-being."

Lauren put them in matching bud vases. "This way, they can look at each other without crowding."

"No comment," Dan said.

A car and driver were waiting for them when they left the building. On the seat, Lauren found two more roses. "In case you already miss the other two," Dan explained.

Their first stop was a very romantic lounge, where they perched on high stools around the jet black grand piano. The waiter arrived to take their orders. "We'll have San Pellegrino," Dan said, without asking Lauren. "I hope it's ok with you, but as it's going to be a long evening, I thought we'd start off slowly."

Before she could respond, the waiter returned with a large bottle of mineral water and two glasses. Beside the sparkling water were two more white roses. Lauren did not know what to say. The smile of delight on Dan's face told her that he was enjoying this.

"Did you buy out the florist?"

"Shh. The set's about to start. No talking," Dan said, winking conspiratorially.

The set was typical piano bar fare, all American standards. The pianist had her own renditions, taking liberties with the tempos and the melodies, singing the familiar tunes with a sultry voice. A bassist, who added his own improvisations to the songs, backed her. Lauren loved every minute of it. She was a sucker for piano music of any kind, and had told Dan how delighted she was that the concert they attended on their first date featured an incredibly talented classical piano prodigy.

They sipped their mineral water, enjoying the music and the intimacy of sitting so close to the performer. Dan placed his hand on hers. He turned towards her and smiled, without letting go.

The pianist announced that there would be only one more song before the set ended. She began playing *Happy Birthday* and Dan sang right along. He had a beautiful voice. The waiters, who had gathered to contribute their voices, stopped after a few bars. Even the pianist gave him the floor.

When the song ended, Dan signaled to the waiter that it was time to leave. After paying the bill, they returned to the waiting car. Lauren was half-expecting to find more roses on the seat, but there were still only two. She added the ones from the piano bar, glad that they were in water picks to keep them fresh.

The drive to the restaurant took about 20 minutes, during which time Dan again reached over to hold Lauren's hand. She was beginning to realize that he was not much of a talker. And she could not think of anything important enough to say to break the silence.

Dan had picked one of the most exclusive restaurants in Chicago for their meal. Once more, he ordered for them both. He chose the tasting menu, accompanied by different wines for each course. By now, Lauren anticipated the roses that came with the bottle of mineral water at the start of their meal. She smiled broadly when the waiter placed them on the table. Dan grinned as he watched her.

The appetizer was the most unusual presentation of caviar that Lauren had ever seen. The roe was served on top of crushed ice in a glass cone. The cone itself sat inside a miniature fish bowl, complete with what must have been a very cold and confused gold fish. It was bizarre eating above a moving target. The chilled champagne that accompanied the appetizer helped her ignore the live element of the serving piece.

The next course was a foie gras and quail terrine, served with tempura gherkins and butter lettuce. Lauren was thankful for the small portions. A chilled red wine, unexpectedly cold but the perfect balance to the room temperature dish, accompanied the paté. Before the next course, the waiter brought small liqueur glasses filled with tart passion fruit sorbet, to cleanse the palette.

The meat course featured lamb in three ways: stuffed into millefeuilles pastry, crisply fried as lamb sausage and elegantly presented as two succulent lamb ribs marinated in mint tea. Lauren broke her rule of avoiding white wine to sip the glass that accompanied this plate. It was dry and crisp and bordered on bubbly.

Dan said little throughout the meal. He appeared to savor each small plate, appreciating the presentation as much as the taste. He tried each glass of wine that came, then offered the rest to Lauren. She declined. With a glass for each course, it was too much alcohol for her. Besides, she was so enjoying the food that the wine seemed almost superfluous.

The dessert course was as extravagant as the others were. It was hard to decide which was more decadent, the dark chocolate ravioli served with cranberry-mango mousse or the Canadian ice wine, presented in glasses of ice wrapped in linen napkins.

"I am truly overwhelmed, Dan. This meal has been spectacular." She paused for the waiter to clear their plates and to bring their coffees.

"Would you like the cheese course?" he asked.

Lauren and Dan shook their heads. "No thank-you," answered Dan. I think we've had our fill. Compliments to the chef. It was an outstanding meal."

They sat, quietly finishing the ice wine and sipping their coffee. Dan again had his hand over Lauren's. She wondered whether he was tongue-tied or whether he really was a man more comfortable with actions than with words.

En route to their next stop, Lauren checked on her growing collection of roses. There were now six in the car. Each time she looked at them, Dan smiled again. The look on his face was that of a little boy who had done something that made him feel really proud. Which of her friends had said that all men were boys?

Lauren did not know what to expect when the driver pulled up to the Hyatt Hotel. She looked questioningly at Dan, who again only smiled. He guided her to the elevator and touched the button for the top floor. The hostess greeted them, checking the reservation before showing them to a table beside the window. The spectacular view of downtown Chicago greeted them. The server appeared. Lauren was not surprised to find two more roses on his tray. That would make ten, so far.

They did not stay long at the lounge. After one more cup of coffee – decaf this time – they headed back to the car. It was already past midnight and Lauren wondered what more could be on the agenda. Her friends were at the age where they were usually home in bed by 11 and on nights like this, she understood why. Dan had picked her up at 6 and they had been driving, eating, and drinking ever since. She was enjoying her time with Dan, but the wine was making her drowsy and the noise in the lounge made conversation difficult. Or would have, had she and Dan been inclined to talk. He spent most of his time holding her hand, alternating his gaze between her and the view.

The next stop was Dan's. The floating home was dark when they walked down the pier. When Dan opened the door for her, he turned on the dimmer lights, keeping the interior fairly dark. After guiding Lauren to the chaise longue, he disappeared for a few moments. He returned with several packages of varying sizes. He set them down while he lit some candles and turned on some music.

Lauren looked at him, surprised. "Dan, this is wonderful. But you did not have to go to all this trouble. The roses alone would have been a beautiful gift."

"That may be. You know, I was looking for a card for you and couldn't find one. They were all wrong. Either too sarcastic or too Hallmarky sentimental. But one had some words I like: 'On your birthday, I celebrate the day you came into my life.' Please don't deny me the fun of your birthday. It's a treat for me, too."

He handed her the smallest of the boxes. Lauren opened it to find a pair of beautiful pearl earrings. The Mikimoto 'M' emblazoned the box. "Don't say a word. Just keep going," Dan said, handing her the second package.

Its shape was a give-away. "Hmmm, I wonder what this could be," Lauren teased. Still, she smiled when she saw the two roses inside. "Now I've got a dozen," she said. "Thank-you. I'll reunite them all and look after them as you asked."

"I've saved the best for last, Lauren. I am sure you realize by now that I am not much of a talker. I just find it easier to show than to tell. Of course, you knew that the day we met at the lake..." She unwrapped the last box. Inside, she found a beautiful parchment envelope. Lauren pulled out the stationery inside. Dan had printed his version of a rain check, "Lauren is entitled to spend as many nights with me as she wants. No expiration date. Ever."

Lauren reached up to Dan, stretching to put her arms around him. The lounger tipped backwards in the process. Dan struggled to right them before falling on top of her. They both laughed. "It really would be more comfortable upstairs."

Lauren and Alan Forester convinced Jeanine to take on a short contract with the organization to work on the APRA conference program. Lauren was glad to have her friend back at work, even if it was only briefly. Jeanine had agreed, subject to being able to continue her twice-weekly baby cuddling shifts at the hospital. Caroline had started to accompany her and Jeanine did not want to disappoint either her friend or the babies. Or herself, she admitted. She looked forward to the volunteer shifts as a way to mark the time and to remember to breathe.

"There are only two things you absolutely must do between now and our next session," her therapist always said at the end of each short hour. "Breathe in and breathe out. Everything else is optional." That philosophy would certainly have helped when she was mourning Henry. She tried to remember it whenever she was stressed.

Lauren and Jeanine put the finishing touches on the program. This year, they provided attendees the option of downloading the schedule onto their Blackberrys. It meant more work, but they hoped it would cut down on paper.

The timing of the conference always presented a challenge for Lauren, as the autumn date was just after the publication deadline of the third quarter edition of the APRA Journal. In fact, each fall, the journal featured a special section on the upcoming event. Lauren put in long hours to meet both timelines. She did most of her work on the conference at the APRA headquarters and kept the journal files on her home computer. She was constantly copying files onto a memory stick that she carried back and forth. If she did not keep both computers synchronized, she was in real trouble.

She saw little of Dan during October. He knew that she was working long hours and tried not to disturb her. Around 7:00 p.m. one evening, Lauren replied to one of Dan's brief emails, saying that she was calling it quits for the day. About an hour later, the concierge at her condominium called up to her apartment. "There's a man here who says he has a delivery for you. His name is Dan Deeden, I think. Should I let him up? I didn't know you were expecting anything."

Lauren started laughing. "Please do," she instructed, when she realized that Dan was using his email moniker, Dandy Dan. She ran her hands through her hair and pinched her cheeks for some color. It was all she had time for while Dan rode the elevator to her floor.

"I thought you would be too tired to cook." Dan walked in carrying an insulated cooler bag. "Just sit and relax while I set this up." He had prepared an entire picnic, complete with checkered tablecloth for her table and real china, stemware and silverware. "I hope you don't mind, but I was tired of eating alone." Dan poured the omnipresent sparkling water into tumblers and some red wine into goblets.

Lauren was too hungry to talk. Besides, by now she realized that Dan took his meals seriously and conversation was not on the menu. She thoroughly enjoyed the large Cobb salad, lightly dressed with Dan's own vinaigrette. She smiled when she bit into a huge chuck of blue cheese. It reminded her of the first meal she had eaten at his home - pasta gorgonzola. He had a real nose for smelly cheeses, no irony intended.

In deference to waistlines and arteries, Dan had substituted turkey bacon for the real thing. "See how I counteracted the cheese, Lauren?" he smiled. He gave her another one of his proud little boy smiles. She was learning how to elicit them and how to respond. All she had to do was smile back and he was happy.

The picnic even included dessert. "After all that protein, you deserve a treat." Dan pulled a bar of dark chocolate from the cooler and broke it into bite-sized pieces. He set a small plate of dried fruit between them and they nibbled contentedly. "Sorry that I couldn't bring decaf, but if you let me into your kitchen, I can fix that, too."

"No, let me do it." Lauren made the coffee while Dan cleared the table and repacked the cooler. He was sitting and staring out at the lake when she returned.

"It's so beautiful here. You know, I love living where I do because it's an oasis of calm right in the middle of the city. But you have a completely different perspective here. I can't decide which is better."

"Why does one have to be better? Think how lucky we are that we can enjoy them both." Lauren served the decafs. "It's so good to sit down without a computer in front of me. And the meal was delicious. I have not been eating properly and you are right, I would have devoured whatever I found in the refrigerator had you not shown up. Thank-you so much."

"How are you doing with your deadlines?"

"I know that everything will get done. It always does. And I am thrilled that Jeanine is back working on the conference with me. We work so well together, because we've been doing the program for so many years." Lauren sipped her coffee and then reached out to touch Dan's hand. "But I haven't been sleeping well. Call it boiling brain, but it is hard to turn everything off when I finally fall into bed. You will laugh, but one night, I dreamt about a gigantic pneumatic tube running from my home office to the APRA. It kept spewing things out at both ends and I could not turn it off. Sort of *The Sorcerer's Apprentice* redux."

"Well, at least your nightmares have a comedic side to them." He brought her hand up to his lips and kissed it. "Cinderella, I have to go. I do not want to, but you have to work tomorrow and I want you to have your beauty rest. Not that you need it, mind you. But you know what I mean."

He stood, gathered up the cooler and his coat and walked to the door. Lauren kissed him lightly before letting him out. By the time Dan reached the lobby, she was preparing for bed. She quickly fell asleep, thinking about what a good man Dan was.

Lauren and Jeanine flew down to Phoenix on the same flight. The Arizona heat hit them the moment they got off the plane. Even mid-morning, it was almost 90 degrees. By the time they arrived at the hotel, they were eager to shower and change into lighter clothing. Of course, the air conditioning in the hotel was positively chilling.

I never thought I'd attend another one of these," Jeanine said, looking around when they met again at the hotel restaurant. "What will all those people think who said goodbye to me at that wonderful luncheon last year? Will they take back their words of praise?"

"Don't be silly, Jeanine. You know they will all be glad to see you again. And that you will have to tell your Africa story about a thousand times. Maybe we could have scheduled a presentation for you during the conference."

"You know, stopping work so abruptly taught me a lot. At first, I was anxious about missing the routine – not to mention the income – I had at the APRA. Then, after I told the Who Don'ts, and you and I had our talk, it tipped the balance from fear to excitement. You know what they say: 'Once you start talking about it, it's a reality.' I can't explain it, but I was afraid you would all think me a complete flake for just taking off like that."

Lauren listened to her friend, still dressed in black. She had been wrong about Africa introducing color into Jeanine's life. At least wrong in the literal sense. It had certainly given her friend a renewed self-confidence.

"I wondered how I would get by on the reduced pension from the APRA. But you know, when I was in Africa, I realized just how wealthy we all are over here. Even the poorest people here have clean water and free education and relative safety. They can get access to health care, and I count the APRA as significantly responsible when I say that. I know there are horrid problems related to poverty, but Lauren, they don't hold a candle to what goes on over there." Jeanine stopped talking and looked at the menu.

"I mean most of the entrées on this menu cost more than the monthly wages of the people I met. And yet, they have something we don't."

"What's that?" Lauren asked.

"This incredible spirit. The belief that things will improve. That their ancestors are looking out for them and will sustain them. That the day-to-day difficulties are not important. I envy them that. That is probably the biggest reason why I will go back on another trip. I want to help, but I also want to learn more."

"You make me feel almost guilty about my next little trip. Dan suggested that he meet me here when the conference ends so that we can spend some time together in Scottsdale. He's flying down on Friday."

"Lauren, you devil, you! Why didn't you tell me before?" Jeanine looked genuinely delighted for her friend. "I didn't tell you what I did about Africa to make you feel guilty. Of course you should spend time with him."

"My late mother-in-law used to tell me that guilt should be reserved for sins. She would say that I should be feeling remorse." Lauren saw that Jeanine was shaking her head and frowning. "OK, no remorse either. Besides, a little sinning with Dan should be fun."

Lauren and Dan spent a much extended weekend in Scottsdale. As a golfer, Dan was in paradise. He had booked an early morning tee time for their first day together, not just to beat the heat, but also to give Lauren the chance to sleep in. The conference had been exhausting, physically and emotionally. On the Thursday before the AGM, they held the traditional luncheon with TLC. It had been unsettling not to see John Bell-Kingsley there. Thankfully, no-one asked Lauren about the reading at the funeral. Still, she felt uncomfortable hearing the banter about John and his relationships with many of the people around the table. "I miss his presence," was all she contributed to the conversation.

Dan played golf every day. After catching up on her sleep on the first day, Lauren used the next morning to visit the resort's spa. She returned to the room so relaxed that she promptly fell asleep again, waking up only when she heard Dan come in from his game. "Don't move," he said, when she smiled up at him. He checked that the 'Do Not Disturb' sign was on the door. "I'm a little tired myself after 18 holes." Lauren pulled back the bedcover for him to join her. Her skin was still oily from her massage.

On the day they were to leave, Dan shot his best game yet. Lauren spent the morning on some retail therapy, then met Dan for a late lunch before heading to the airport. "Too bad we couldn't get an even later check-out," Dan commented. "I could have used another nap."

"You're so bad," Lauren teased, enjoying the rare bit of repartee from Dan. She handed him a package from the pro shop. "I couldn't resist getting these for you." Dan opened the box to find a new black leather golf glove and a golf towel boasting the name of the renowned course he had played. "You know, a man can never have too many things to wipe his hands, especially when they're all oily from other things."

When Gary and I were teenagers, we always got together on January 1. It was a day to relax, usually spent just hanging around his house. Gary's parents always welcomed me, which was great because the apartment I shared with my mother was not conducive to having guests. Friends of Gary's and mine would drop by on New Year's Day, too. It became something of a ritual with all of us.

Usually, I went out with someone else on New Year's Eve and Gary was too unsure of his status with me to protest. It worked two ways. I always looked for a date because I never really believed that Gary would ask me out. By the time we would broach the subject of New Year's with each other, it was too late to change plans. That's why we decided to spend the beginning of the year together, so that we could start on the right foot.

The feeling of good beginnings has stayed with me all these years. That is why I chose to write my journal today. And I realize that I may not have written from Virgin Gorda before, but that does not mean I have not visited. A few years back, I was here on a Windjammer Cruise. Even that was not the first time I had been to this corner of paradise. Richard and I were here twice, once alone and another time with the kids. Jason was only a baby when we visited as a family, which reminds me of how long ago it was.

When Dan and I started talking about escaping the Chicago winter, I suggested Virgin Gorda right away. He was not hard to convince, even though there is no golf course on the island. It took him very little time to find out about Mahogany Run, an 18-hole championship caliber club on nearby St. Thomas, in the US Virgins. It is only a short ferry ride away. He is so accommodating that way. Nothing seems to upset his equilibrium. He takes everything in stride. His favorite expression is, 'It is what it is.' He really means that.

What can I say about Dan? In some ways, he remains a mystery to me. He still does not talk much, but that's ok. It is really his actions that count. He is a man of great empathy and integrity, and that means so much to me.

How did he ever survive to the age of 60 without marrying? I joked about it at first. Eventually, he told me. While he never had a wedding, he did have two long and stable live-in relationships. "Don't think that because I've never married, I've been alone. I haven't." The first woman he lived with had died of breast cancer. They had been together for 12 years, raising her child from a previous marriage. Not only did Dan mourn this woman, but he also felt helpless and saddened by the loss of the girl, when her maternal grandparents moved her to another state to live with them after her mother's death.

Dan had no legal rights because he had not adopted her. He chose not to get into a legal battle over her, because he was not sure he could raise her on his own. After a few years, they lost touch, but then she invited him to her wedding a few years back. He is now a proud self-appointed grandfather to baby Daniel, named after him. He was so touched by that gesture. I have seen the photos from little Daniel's christening and Dan is just beaming.

After a significant hiatus of what he refers to as self-imposed celibacy, Dan got involved with another woman. This time, she was considerably younger than he was. Not unlike the situation I had with John Bell-Kinsgley, they had almost a mentoring relationship, with sex thrown in as a bonus. They lived together for three years, and then parted amicably when Dan began to wind down his business interests just as the woman's career was taking off. They still exchange Christmas cards, but that is all that is left of their relationship.

Dan was alone for some time before we met. Deirdre told me that he dated from time to time. He was always being fixed up and asked to fill the man's seat at dinner parties. He was a catch, although he did not seem to realize that. But, luckily for me, he never had a real interest in any of the women he met, either in Chicago or at the lake in Wisconsin. After a while, his golf friends began to tease him about his bachelor status. And their wives continued to push Dan to settle down again, preferably with one of their friends. I am not sorry to disappoint them.

He was never able to decide which view he preferred, so Dan kept his floating home and I still have the condominium. In some ways, the arrangement is perfect. I'm still working for the APRA, although I'm down to half-time now, partly at Dan's suggestion and partly because it's time for me to finally do some of the things I've put off for so long. That includes savoring this wonderful relationship Dan and I have.

When I have a deadline or lots of work to do, Dan stays on the houseboat. He does not like me to call it that, because he tells me that a houseboat and a floating home are completely different. The former is made to move, while the latter is permanently moored. But it is my journal and my shorthand, so don't tell. His absence allows me to work my own crazy hours, without feeling obligated to spend time with him. And then, when we do get together, it is like a special reunion all over again. Maybe this is the relationship I have always been looking for. It allows me to be independent and to have a fulfilling relationship with a loving man, at the same time. I never believed this was even possible.

Emma and Jason seem genuinely happy for me. They have met Dan, of course, and have an easy relationship with him. They are not quite buddy-buddy, but then, I never expected them to be. Dan does not pretend to father them. He respects them as young adults and relates to them accordingly and appropriately. They joined us here for Christmas, which was a surprise gift from Dan. He flew them down here and arranged their stays without letting on at all. What can I say?

Dan has not met Richard yet, although I suppose that is inevitable. One of these days, there will be a major event in the kids' lives that Richard and I will both attend. Of course, we will each bring our mate. I will finally meet Richard's wife. And Richard will meet Dan, whether he is my husband or not.

It is interesting to think about that. Marriage, that is. It is something we talk about from time to time, but for now, it is not high on either of our priority lists. Perhaps it never will be. Or maybe when Dan and I both completely retire, it might make more sense. For the moment, we are committed to each other and are fine with the arrangements as they stand.

A year after we met, Dan surprised me with a beautiful emerald ring. The stone is enormous. "Just because I want you to have it," he said when he handed me the box. "It doesn't mean anything other than that I think you are as rare and as beautiful as it is." He does not speak much, but when he does, he has such a way with words! I wear the ring on my right hand.

When the Who Don'ts saw it, we had a huge discussion about bling. We agreed that women of a certain age can wear big jewelry without looking ostentatious, whereas younger women wearing the same jewels might look flashy. Of course, Melanie felt it was unfair that she had to wait for the bounty, but we reminded her that it would look wrong with her doorman's uniform.

She is still working at that job and is as happy as a clam. She now spends time on art for herself, rather than teaching it to earn money. She has shown some of her works in cafés around town, and she even had a small show at a gallery in Old Town. It seems as if her day job releases some kind of creative energy for her and we all think that ultimately, her pen and ink drawings will become her primary source of livelihood. She is not so sure.

Dan and I continue to spend a lot of time with Deirdre. She is still in the throes of legal battles because of her split from Russell. At first, I was not sure whether Dan would be comfortable with her, as he was so close to Russ. But Dan set me straight when I broached the subject. "If Russ expects me to side with him when he's behaved so abominably, he doesn't know me as well as I thought he did. I cannot continue to count him as a friend. If he could cheat on Deirdre, who is such a dear woman, how can I respect him? And if I can't respect him, how can I call him a friend?" That is what I mean about his integrity.

I wondered how the other two men in Dan's long-standing golf foursome would react. It was an even split. One man stays in touch with Russ and avoids Dan and the other does the opposite. The former foursome does not golf together any more. I feel bad for Dan about that, but he does not seem to mind. "There are friends for a reason and friends for a season and friends for a lifetime," he tells me. "I always thought that Russ was one of the rare ones in the lifetime category, but I was wrong. I realize our friendship should have ended a long time ago. He wasn't honest with me and that's no way for friends to treat each other."

I wish I could be so calm about friends coming and going. But he is right, you know. I now realize that it is ok to let people go when their reason or their season has passed. That is an insight from Dan that I really value. It has let me realize that I could never resurrect my relationship with Gary. And that's ok. I have learned a lot from Dan, as you can tell. I admire his approach to life and really am happy to be part of it. He has a plaque hanging in his office that reads, 'It will all work out in the end. If it hasn't worked out, it's not the end.' I think our relationship is one of the things that will really work out in the end. I mean, it is going well already, but we are not at the end yet.

So we spend time with Deirdre, trying to support her through her *War of the Roses* divorce from Russ. It is a good thing they never had kids, or he would fight her over them, too. I saw her going through all the tears and the self-doubts that I experienced when Richard and I split. And although I remember how much I hated hearing those silly platitudes, I admit that I did tell her to take baby steps and to live one day at a time. And, even though she told me she would do something drastic if I uttered any of those expressions again, she did listen. And she is slowly coming out of the misery stage. She tells Dan and me that she is relishing the anger phase. She walks around, cursing like a sailor whenever Russ's name comes up. She says that it feels terrific to vent after all those years of silent acceptance. She will be ok, my dear old friend Deirdre. I know she will.

And the others? Jeanine continues to commute, if that is the word, between Chicago and Africa. To no-one's surprise but her own, one of the charities she previously volunteered for offered her a paid position. She is now the inter-agency liaison, working to coordinate resources and efforts to raise the literacy and education rates of young girls. It is not an easy job but she is giving it her all and I know she will make a difference. Her work takes her to different parts of Africa and she has visited countries that I could not find on a map. Then again, geography was never my strong suit.

When she is in Chicago, Jeanine continues to cuddle babies. It's ironic that the hospital work is now her only volunteer commitment. Caroline finds it amusing that she is now the regular on the ward, with Jeanine only dropping in every few months for what she calls her baby fix. Incidentally, Jeanine still wears black. She says it's a decision based largely on economics now. As if she cannot afford a new wardrobe.

I think the baby cuddling has made a world of difference to Caroline. And it has rubbed off on Dave, too. So much so, that they now volunteer as surrogate grandparents for kids in their neighborhood living far from extended family. It is nothing formal, but they have let it be known that they will babysit and give parents respite from time to time.

Last year, they even held a sleep-over for a six-year-old whose parents had to go out-of-town at the last moment. Caroline was beside herself preparing for the three little girls who arrived with great bravado, armed with sleeping bags and DVDs and stuffed animals. You would have thought that Caroline and Dave were entertaining royalty. We heard all about it at the next Who Don'ts dinner, where we saw the photos Caroline took of the giggling girls. One shot showed Dave trying to teach them how to bake muffins for breakfast. There was flour everywhere, but the best part was the look on Dave's face. Priceless.

And lastly, there is Hélène. She retired from her job as headmistress last year. I think she was worn out trying to instill some refinement into her charges. She may still have the opportunity, though, as she was invited to sit on the Board of the School and she accepted after a hiatus of about six months. That place is as much in her blood as her Gallic charm. You should hear her talk from the other side of the table now. Even though she clearly can empathize with the new head of school, she is much freer to voice her opinions than she was before. And she takes full advantage of her director status. Who knows? She may yet get the girls to behave like the sophisticated young women she wants them to be.

What is interesting about Hélène is how she finally turned her passion for fashion into a reality. She is so clever. She travels back and forth to France several times a year. Through her connections there, she is able to buy samples and over-runs from all the major fashion houses. These are the real thing, not designs shipped to China to be mass-produced. And because she carries two passports, one from the USA and one from the EU, she can bring things back here quite easily. I do not really understand the tariffs involved, but it doesn't matter.

Hélène holds house fashion parties for a fairly exclusive list of women, many of them mothers of girls at the Chicago French School. Occasionally, they even bring their daughters along. Thankfully, the Who Don'ts are the first to see her collections and we buy from her as soon as she returns. It works beautifully. We have all moved up several notches on the fashion scale, thanks to her.

Dan always laughs when I tell him another shipment is arriving. He considers the whole thing somewhat clandestine, although I know he is just giving me a hard time about it. He is the first to compliment me on my purchases, so I know he also gets a kick out of Hélène's entrepreneurial fashion adventures.

We had all the Who Don'ts over for a holiday celebration early in December, before we came down to Virgin Gorda. Although we had not planned it that way, each of us wore an outfit that we had bought from Hélène. She was delighted. It's funny that that evening we were six women and only two men. Dave almost did not come, but changed his mind when he heard that he would not be the only man present. Hélène gave him a huge hug at the door. She squeezed him extra hard, explaining that she had to be sure he really existed. He looked at her as if she were crazy, but hugged back. After all the years that the Who Don'ts had known each other, it was, in fact, the first time they had met.

It is funny that when I held my housewarming party at my condominium, I worried that there would be more women than men. I guess nothing has changed. No, that is not quite true. A lot has changed in the past few years and I suspect that more changes are on the way. I just do not know what they are yet. The best part is that I no longer stress over the uncertainties. Dan has his favorite expressions. I have mine and it sums things up perfectly: 'When nothing is certain, everything is possible.'

From the sequel, **The Ladies Who Still Don't Lunch**, *available only on Amazon.com as a paperback and on world-wide amazon sites as an e-book.*

Only Jeanine wore black to the funeral. She did so not because she was in mourning; her husband had died many years earlier. She wore black because since losing her husband, she wore only that color.

The new widow was Deirdre. It was her husband, Russell, who was in the coffin at the front of the chapel. A sudden and massive heart attack killed him instantly. Deirdre was still surprised that he was dead; wasn't he healthy enough to fight her viciously over their divorce settlement? Or perhaps the stress was what did him in. His intransigence meant that when Russell died, they did not have a formal separation agreement. Legally, that meant they were still married, and as they were childless and Russ had no other close family, that meant that Deirdre inherited Russell's entire estate. Her mind drifted from the eulogy, as she wondered how much of the inheritance she would have to deplete to cover Russell's legal expenses for fighting the divorce. Or whether the lawyer would write off the account as a bad debt, out of sympathy. Given her experience with this attorney, she very much doubted it.

Deirdre's daydreaming was interrupted when she heard her name called. The minister had concluded his remarks and invited Deirdre to the podium. She didn't feel comfortable speaking at Russell's funeral, but her friends had convinced her to say something. Now that she felt their eyes on her as she approached the lectern, she was even more uncertain about where to start.

"My friends," she began, peering first at each one of the five women in the front row, then at the rest of the guests, "we are gathered here to mourn the loss of Russell. I never imagined that I would be here, talking about him in the past tense, but life deals us strange hands to play. I did not imagine I would become a widow, and I am reeling from my new status.

"As most of you know, Russ and I were in the midst of protracted divorce negotiations when he died. I cannot stand here and pretend to be a grieving widow. Nor can I pretend that Russ was my sainted husband. Neither of those statements would be true."

Deirdre did not have notes; she spoke from her heart. "Despite everything, I cannot state that Russ was a bad person who deserved to die so suddenly. I loved him, at least at first, and I was so happy to marry him. I wanted what many of my women friends did: a husband, a family, a future... The whole white picket fence scenario. But Russ did not, apparently.

"He was unfaithful throughout our marriage, and perhaps even while we were dating and engaged. I don't know. I do know that, although I wanted kids and was initially disappointed that we did not have a family, I am grateful that I do not have to explain to any children that their father's behavior was so disrespectful, so hurtful and so wrong.

"It is ironic that Russ died before we divorced. He leaves me a widow, rather than an ex-wife. It is strange that his death reattaches me to him, even after I finally began to live my life without him these past few years.

"But this is his funeral, and my goal is not to further malign him. So, for the moment, I will ignore his behavior towards me, and admit that he died too soon. No-one deserves that."

Deirdre did not add a wish for Russ to rest in peace. She returned to the pew and was only vaguely aware when the service ended shortly afterwards. There weren't many people there. Most of those who knew Deirdre and Russell also knew about their bitter legal battles and were too uncomfortable to attend his funeral. The few others in the small chapel were either only vaguely familiar or completely unknown to her. The ones she thought she might know were no doubt Russ's work colleagues. The others, not surprisingly, were women whom Deirdre did not recognize. Perhaps they were some of Russ's past indiscretions.

Nothing would surprise Deirdre at this point. Not her status as a widow and not the absurd call she received shortly after Russ died. A woman phoned to ask for details of the funeral service. When Deirdre asked who she was, the woman responded, "Oh, I thought you knew that I was Russ's special friend. He spoke about you to me, so I assumed that the reverse was also true. I guess not, right?" Deirdre was astounded when the woman asked if she could bring her children to the funeral. She explained that they were very fond of Russ and that he treated them like his own. Dumbstruck, Deirdre told the caller that children would not be welcome. After she hung up, she wondered what the woman looked like and whether she would attend the funeral, even without her children. Perhaps she was one of the strangers at the service.

Only Deirdre and her close women friends bundled into the limousine heading to the cemetery. The graveside service was mercifully brief. Afterwards, Hélène invited the Ladies Who Don't Lunch to her private club to decompress. The club, named The Feminary, was tucked in among the older buildings just north of the Loop. Whenever they went there, The Ladies Who Don't Lunch enjoyed the hush that permeated the dining room and the small lounges scattered over several floors of the building. The Feminary was the perfect cocoon for the mood enveloping Deirdre.

She entered the building with her friends, where the décor and ambiance immediately calmed her. Deirdre glanced at the reflection of the women in one of the mirrors along the entry wall. Who were they? How could Deirdre have made it through Russ's death and funeral without them?

Evelyn Lazare is a retired health care executive. *The Ladies Who Don't Lunch* is her first novel. Evelyn lives in Steveston, British Columbia, Canada, where she has just published a sequel to *The Ladies Who Don't Lunch*, called *The Ladies Who Still Don't Lunch*. She is currently working on another novel. You can contact Evelyn at the.who.donts@evelynhl.com.